# AL UBELL'S ENERGY-SAVING GUIDE FOR HOMEOWNERS

# AL UBELL'S ENERGY-SAVING GUIDE FOR HOMEOWNERS

## by Alvin Ubell and George Merlis

WARNER BOOKS

A Warner Communications Company

Warner Books Edition
Copyright © 1980 by Jeffrey Weiss, Alvin Ubell and George Merlis
All rights reserved.
Warner Books, Inc., 75 Rockefeller Plaza, New York, New York 10019

**W** A Warner Communications Company

Printed in the United States of America
First printing: October 1980
10 9 8 7 6 5 4 3 2 1
Produced by Color Book Design, Inc.
Designed by R.J. Luzzi
Illustrated by Craig Carl
Cover design by Gene Light
Cover photos by Bill Cadge
Editorial Assistance—Barbara Frontera

The advice in this book in intended to suggest possible solutions only. The authors and publishers cannot guarantee absolute success. To guard against damage, we recommend care.

# A Jeffrey Weiss book

**Library of Congress Cataloging in Publication Data**

Ubell, Alvin, 1933–
    Al Ubell's Energy-saving guide for home owners.

    Includes index.
    1. Dwellings—Energy conservation.   I. Merlis,
George, 1940–    joint author.   II.  Good Morning
America (Television program)   III. Title.   IV. Title:
Energy-saving guide.
TJ163.5.D86U23        644        80-17003
ISBN 0-446-97666-0 (U.S.A.)
ISBN 0-446-97763-2 (Canada)

For Estelle and Sue.

When Al Ubell and George Merlis first asked me to do an introduction for their new *Energy Saving Guide*, I thought, "Oh no, not another complicated handyman manual that takes a Ph.D. to understand." I've read and tested many of these books before and they only ended up in my yearly garage sale. Needless to say, I wasn't looking forward to spending my free weekend reading about energy problems. But guess what? Not only did I read it cover to cover but I found myself running about our home having fun testing their various money saving ideas about heating, cooking, washing and so on. That weekend I became aware of how my family was wasting energy—but thanks to Al Ubell this book makes it easy to do something about it.

# A Handy Guide
# To What's Inside

**I. Introduction: "What Difference Do I Make?"** 1

**II. Where Your Energy Dollar Goes** 3

**III. What's Your E.Q.?** 5

*Your Energy Audit* 5

—Heating 5

—Insulation 7

—Windows and Doors 8

—Water Heating and Usage 8

—Air Conditioning and Ventilation 8

—Lighting 9

—Television 9

—The Kitchen 9

—The Laundry 10

—The Bathroom 10

—Outside the House 10

—Bonuses 10

*How Well Did You Score?* 11

**IV. Home Heating** 13

*Insulation* 13

—R-Values 14

—Types of Insulation 16

● Caveat Emptor 17

—Where to Insulate 18

—Vapor Barriers 22

—Installing Insulation Yourself 24

● Insulating Your Attic 24

● Insulating an Exterior Wall 29

- Insulating an Unfinished Masonry Wall  30
- Insulating Door and Window Frames  31
- Insulating Above a Cold Crawlspace  31
- Insulating Unused Rooms  33

—*Windows and Doors*  34
- Inspect Your Windows  35
- Broken Window Pane  36
- Broken, Loose or Missing Window Latches  38
- Loose Sashes  39
- Loose Frames  40
- Lack of Weatherstripping  40
- Lack of Caulking  42
- Shades, Blinds, Drapes and Shutters  46
- Storm Windows and Doors  49
- Doors  54
- Weatherstripping Doors  55

*Outside Your House*  59

—Roofing and Siding  59

—Landscaping  61

*How Do You Heat?*  62

—Turn Down That Thermostat  63

—Use a Humidifier  66

—Making Your Old Furnace More Efficient—
By Yourself  68
- Remove Obstructions  68
- Lubricate Motors  70
- Change Old Air Vents  71
- Check and Repair Heating Ducts  71
- Change or Clean Clogged Filters  71
- Pitch Your Radiators Properly  73
- Set the Cutoff Valve  73

● Check and Replace Air Valves  74
● Bleed Radiators  75

—Having Your Old Furnace Made More
Efficient—Jobs for a Professional  76
● Have a Tuneup  76
● Derating  77
● Get an Automatic Flue Damper  77
● Have Hanging Baffles Installed  78
● Install a Return Air Duct  78

*Your Fireplace*  80
● Close That Damper  81
● Close Off the Fireplace  82
● Glass Fireplace Doors  82
● Wood-Stove Fireplace Insert  82
—Wood-Burning Stoves  83
● Wood Stove Safety  86
—How Economical Is It?  88

V. **The Worst Possible Conditions: Surviving
Without Fuel in an Emergency**  91
*Plan Ahead*  91
*When It Happens*  92
—Emergency Lighting  94
—Exposure Treatment  94

VI. **Feeding Energy-Hungry Mouths: Your
Appliances**  97
*The Code of the West—and East, North and South
Getting More Efficiency from Your Appliances*  101
—the Water Heater  101

—Cool, Man, Cool: Air Conditioning and
  Ventilation 106
  ● Tolerating Higher Temperatures 106
  ● Servicing Your Air Conditioner 106
  ● Economy Runs 108
  ● Shut It Off 108
  ● Be a Cool Customer 108
  ● Shade It 108
  ● Be a Fan of a Fan 110
  ● Additional Ventilation 111
  ● Nature's Own 111
—You Light Up My House: Lighting 112
  ● Be Lumen-Wise 112
  ● Fluorescents 113
  ● Here's a Switch 114
  ● Daylight 117
  ● The Shape of Things to Come 117
—If You Can Stand the Heat, Stay in the Kitchen:
  Kitchen and Laundry Appliances 117
  ● Refrigerator 117
  ● Your Range 120
  ● Washing Dishes 120
  ● Monday Is Wash Day?—Laundry Appliances 121
Energy Monitors 122
VII. Uncle Sam Wants You: Tax Credits 125
  How Do I Get the Credit? 126
  Qualifying Energy-Saving Improvements 128
  Renewable Energy Source Credits 128
  Laws Change 128
VIII. Index

# INTRODUCTION

## "What Difference Do I Make?"

If you're like me, you're a victim of spiraling energy prices. In fact, if you live anywhere but in a cave in a nice, warm climate, you've been stung by rapid increases in the cost of oil, natural gas and electricity.

Chances are you're mad enough about those prices—and about the fact that we are being held hostage by the world's energy suppliers—to do something about it. That's why you bought this book.

"What difference do I make?" All the difference in the world! You and I developed wasteful energy habits when fuel and power were cheap. They're not cheap anymore, and it's time for all of us to fight back.

Each of us, working alone, can affect the fate of our society! And, incredibly, we don't have to sacrifice to do it—we can actually *save*! The more efficiently we use our costly fuels, the stronger we are as a nation. And the more dollars we save as individuals.

While the best minds search for energy alternatives, this book contains some answers for now and the foreseeable future. It will save you its purchase price hundreds of times over. How many other books in your home paid for themselves?

But before you begin daydreaming of greenbacks, you have to read the book and follow my recommendations. I know it'll be satisfying for you: Your home will be more comfortable, you'll save money and you'll do your share in reducing our country's energy dependence on foreign powers.

A word of caution: Many of the energy - and money - saving projects I'll tell you about are of the do-it-yourself variety. But some are not; these should only be attempted by trained professionals. I'll clearly indicate which are which, and I can't urge you too strongly to take my advice on this matter. Regardless of how skilled a home handyman you are, DON'T attempt those jobs I identify as professional-only projects. They involve your home heating and electrical systems, and a botched job in these areas can lead to unnecessary fire hazards.

You'll save the cost of the professional worker in the long run, and you'll be a lot more secure in the knowledge the job was done right.

But those jobs that you can do are *easy*! Even if you think of yourself as having ten thumbs, you *can* do these jobs! And you'll love the money you'll save.

**So now, America, go forth and save energy and money.** But before you save, you have to know—

# WHERE YOUR ENERGY DOLLAR GOES

You're paying a lot more for energy of all kinds these days—oil, gas and electricity cost double (and in some cases, nearly triple) what they ran you just a few short years ago. The higher cost of energy is also reflected in the price of everything else you buy—energy-related price hikes have been shooting out of sight recently. (After all, *everyone's* an energy-consumer, including your grocer, delivery man, food packager, even your government—and *everyone's* going to pass on his increased energy costs to you in the form of higher prices.)

But on a direct, personal,

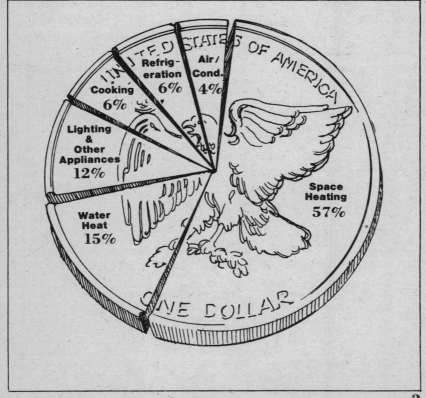

home level, do you know where your energy dollars are going?

The greatest part of your energy budget goes toward keeping that house of yours warm and comfortable. Heating fuels consume about 57 percent of the average family energy budget.

Another fifteen percent pays for the hot water in your shower, bathtub, clothes washer or kitchen sink.

And the remaining 28 percent? That pays for cooking, lighting, running that toaster, the tv, the vacuum cleaner, the hair dryer and the dozens of other appliances we all depend on.

Remember, those are approximate figures. Obviously, if you live in a warm climate, you spend less to heat your house and more to cool it. And if you're one of those self-reliant types with few (or even no) electrical appliances except your house lights, the proportion changes again.

Regardless of the exact dollar figure, however, all of us can make some improvements, save some energy and save some money.

We may have to spend some money to save in the future, but lower fuel bills and lower utility costs will very quickly pay back those expenditures. In fact, you should think of any energy-saving improvements in your home as one-time *investments*—investments virtually guaranteed to pay for themselves many times over! To find out how much you *can* save, you'll need to test yourself to learn—

4

# —WHAT'S YOUR E.Q.?

E.Q.? Energy Quotient! Are you energy-wise or energy-fuelish? Are you a 1,000-hitter or a 100-point energy wastrel?

Here's a way to grade yourself. If you reach 1,000 points on this little energy audit, you've made just about every improvement you can and you lead an extremely energy-conscious existence.

But most of us won't score anywhere near 1,000. We've gotten into some really bad habits over the years, and there's lots of room for improvement in most of our homes and in most of our lives.

So take this test, grade yourself, your home and your lifestyle. And then follow my advice in the book and see how many points you can gain. You might think of it as a game; a game that can pay you big-dollar prizes as you approach the magic 1,000-point mark. And a game that's really *rewarding* to play.

## YOUR ENERGY AUDIT

### HEATING

Usual thermostat setting:

| Winter Day | Possible Points | Your Score |
|---|---|---|
| 74°F | 0 | _____ |
| 73 | 3 | _____ |
| 72 | 6 | _____ |
| 71 | 9 | _____ |
| 70 | 12 | _____ |
| 69 | 15 | _____ |
| 68 | 18 | _____ |
| 67 | 21 | _____ |
| 66 | 24 | _____ |
| 65 | 27 | _____ |
| 64 | 30 | _____ |

| Winter Night | Possible Points | Your Score |
|---|---|---|
| 65°F | 15 | _____ |
| 64 | 18 | _____ |
| 63 | 21 | _____ |
| 62 | 24 | _____ |
| 61 | 27 | _____ |
| 60 | 30 | _____ |

| | Possible Points | Your Score |
|---|---|---|
| You use an electric blanket to allow you to lower thermostat at night. | 6 | _____ |
| You wear two sweaters indoors so you can lower thermostat during the day | 9 | _____ |
| You've installed an automatic flue damper | 30 | _____ |
| Your heating system has been serviced within the last six months | 15 | _____ |
| You change or clean your heating system filters every month | 3 | _____ |
| Your heating ducts have no leaks, or leaks have been taped | 4 | _____ |
| All heating ducts or steam pipes are insulated | 4 | _____ |
| Your oil burner burns without smoke or signs of carbon on its surfaces | 9 | _____ |
| You have a working draft adjuster in your oil burner | 9 | _____ |
| Your gas burner burns with a clear, blue flame | 9 | _____ |
| Your gas burner has an electronic ignition system, not a pilot light | 10 | _____ |
| Your oil burner is a new one with a retention head | 30 | _____ |

| | Possible Points | Your Score |
|---|---|---|
| You use a humidifier during the winter | 9 | _____ |
| Your radiators or air supply registers are not blocked by drapes or furniture and are clean | 27 | _____ |
| You close off rooms not in use and turn off the heat in them | 25 | _____ |
| You keep your fireplace damper shut, or you have glass fireplace doors | 25 | _____ |
| On winter days, you open your drapes on the south side of the house and close them at night to take advantage of radiant heat from the sun | 10 | _____ |

## INSULATION

| | Possible Points | Your Score |
|---|---|---|
| Attic insulation | | |
|     None | −15 | _____ |
|     2″ or R-4 | 0 | _____ |
|     4″ or R-11 | 15 | _____ |
|     6″ or R-19 | 30 | _____ |
|     8″ or R-24 | 45 | _____ |
|     10″ or R-30 | 60 | _____ |
|     12″ or R-38 | 75 | _____ |
| All your insulation has vapor barriers | 15 | _____ |
| Your attic door is insulated | 6 | _____ |
| Insulation in your exterior walls: | | |
|     None | −6 | _____ |
|     3″ or R-11 | 25 | _____ |
| Insulation in crawlspaces | | |
|     None | 0 | _____ |
|     6″ or R-19 | 30 | _____ |
| Your attic and crawlspace are ventilated | 15 | _____ |
| No basement crawlspace | 30 | _____ |
| All outlets and switchplates are insulated | 6 | _____ |
| Your foundation wall is insulated | 30 | _____ |
| Vapor barrier on foundation wall | 9 | _____ |
| You have storm windows | 25 | _____ |
| You have storm doors or a vestibule | 15 | _____ |

# WINDOWS AND DOORS

| | Possible Points | Your Score |
|---|---|---|
| Your windows are not drafty | 30 | _____ |
| Your doors are not drafty | 15 | _____ |
| Cracks at doors, windows and where wood and masonry meet are caulked | 30 | _____ |
| All window glass has full putty | 15 | _____ |
| Broken windows   (deduct for each) | −9 | _____ |
| Double-glazed windows | 25 | _____ |

## WATER HEATING AND USAGE

| | Possible Points | Your Score |
|---|---|---|
| Water heater insulated | 15 | _____ |
| You've set your water heater temperature at: | | |
| 110°F | 12 | _____ |
| 120 | 9 | _____ |
| 130 | 6 | _____ |
| 140 | 3 | _____ |
| 150 | 0 | _____ |
| 160 | −3 | _____ |
| 170 | −6 | _____ |
| 180 | −9 | _____ |
| You drain sediment from water heater every month | 5 | _____ |
| You've installed solar water heater | 44 | _____ |

## AIR CONDITIONING AND VENTILATION

| | Possible Points | Your Score |
|---|---|---|
| Your air-conditioning thermostat is set at: | | |
| 74°F | 0 | _____ |
| 75 | 3 | _____ |
| 76 | 6 | _____ |
| 77 | 9 | _____ |
| 78 | 15 | _____ |
| 79 | 15 | _____ |
| 80 | 18 | _____ |
| No air conditioning | 20 | _____ |

| | Possible Points | Your Score |
|---|---|---|
| You use natural ventilation and wear lightweight clothes in summer | 5 | _____ |
| You close drapes on hot, sunny days | 5 | _____ |
| You close windows and doors on hottest days | 5 | _____ |
| Your air conditioners all have 8 or higher EER (Energy Efficiency Ratios) | | |
| Central System | 9 | _____ |
| Window units—per unit | 1.5 | _____ |
| Your air-conditioning units are shaded or on north side of house | | |
| Central unit | 5 | _____ |
| Window units—per unit | 1 | _____ |
| You have an attic ventilation fan | 15 | _____ |

## LIGHTING

| | | |
|---|---|---|
| You've installed fluorescent lights in kitchen | 15 | _____ |
| All closet lights on auto-switch or timer switches | 8 | _____ |
| You replace multiple low-watt bulbs with single high-watt bulbs for same light value but lower total wattage | 9 | _____ |
| You habitually turn off lights when leaving a room | 15 | _____ |
| You have energy-saving (solid state) dimmer switches (per switch) | 5 | _____ |

## TELEVISION

| | | |
|---|---|---|
| Instant-on tv sets (deduct per set) | −5 | _____ |
| You turn off tv and hi-fi when not in use | 15 | _____ |
| You fall asleep with tv on | −30 | _____ |

## THE KITCHEN

| | | |
|---|---|---|
| Your refrigerator is in a cool spot | 5 | _____ |
| The EER of your refrigerator is above 7 | 9 | _____ |
| You close the refrigerator door quickly, rather than dawdle | 5 | _____ |
| You have a manual-defrost refrigerator | 10 | _____ |

9

| | Possible Pts. | Your Score |
|---|:---:|:---:|
| You defrost it regularly | 5 | _____ |
| You clean the back of the refrigerator | 5 | _____ |
| The refrigerator door gasket fits tightly | 9 | _____ |
| You air-dry dishes rather than use your dishwasher drying cycle | 6 | _____ |
| You have a flow restrictor in your kitchen faucet | 6 | _____ |
| Your gas range has an electronic ignition system, rather than a pilot light | 29 | _____ |
| All the gas burners have a clean, blue flame | 15 | _____ |

## THE LAUNDRY

| | | |
|---|:---:|:---:|
| You wash with cold water | 9 | _____ |
| You use a clothesline, rather than your dryer | 9 | _____ |
| You turn off the iron when you're not using it | 9 | _____ |
| You forget to turn off the iron | − 18 | _____ |

## THE BATHROOM

| | | |
|---|:---:|:---:|
| You shower rather than bathe | 15 | _____ |
| You have a flow restrictor in your shower | 6 | _____ |
| You fix leaky faucets promptly | 15 | _____ |

## OUTSIDE THE HOUSE

| | | |
|---|:---:|:---:|
| Trees and shrubs are placed to allow sun in winter, block wind in cold weather, but shade house in summer | 40 | _____ |

## BONUSES

| | | |
|---|:---:|:---:|
| Installing a clock thermostat with day and night settings | 15 | _____ |
| Installing a clock thermostat with double setback capability | 20 | _____ |

**10**

|  | Possible Points | Your Score |
|---|---|---|
| Installing a heat-producing greenhouse on the south side of the house | 44 | _____ |
| Installing an energy monitor | 45 | _____ |
| Installing a wood-burning stove (if wood is inexpensive in your area) | 55 | _____ |
| Installing a windmill, solar heating and/or cooling, or any other renewable energy source | 150 | _____ |

|  |  |
|---|---|
| **Possible total approx. 1350\*** | **Your total** |

## HOW WELL DID YOU SCORE?

| If your score was | Here's how much you can save on your energy costs |
|---|---|
| 0-99 | 50 to 75 percent |
| 100-199 | 45 to 70 percent |
| 200-299 | 40 to 65 percent |
| 300-399 | 35 to 60 percent |
| 400-499 | 30 to 55 percent |
| 500-599 | 25 to 50 percent |
| 600-699 | 20 to 45 percent |
| 700-799 | 15 to 40 percent |
| 800-899 | 10 to 35 percent |
| 900-999 | 5 to 30 percent |
| 1000 or more | You win a gold star! You've gone about as far as you can go. |

But the chances are you *haven't* gotten to 1,000 points yet, so let's begin with the big energy-eater—

---

\*Possible total will vary from house to house, since points are given for gas furnaces which oil-heated houses won't qualify for and vice versa.

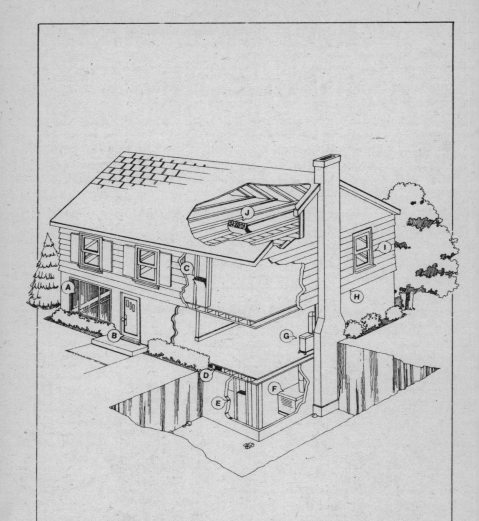

*Your house will save you heating dollars if it has the following:*
*A. Storm windows. B. Storm doors. C. Insulated exterior walls.*
*D. Insulated cellar ceilings or crawlspaces. E. Insulated cellar*
*walls. F. An upgraded, clean furnace. G. A supplementary*
*wood-burning stove. H. Caulking where the foundation meets*
*the siding. I. Caulked and weatherstripped windows. J. An*
*insulated attic.*

# —HOME HEATING
# INSULATION

What do you wear on a cold day? Do you walk outdoors with a thin, threadbare sweater on? If you do, you feel mighty cold. That's because that thin sweater of yours is letting your body heat escape into the cold air.

Now, very few of us walk out on a frigid day dressed like that. Usually we put on something heavier than a skimpy sweater. Maybe we put on a down-filled parka. One of those quilt-like garments can keep us comfortable at very low temperatures. Why? Because the down creates air spaces which prevent our body heat from escaping—it *insulates* our bodies.

Now, if all we've got is that thin sweater, there *is* a way of keeping warmer—and that's by jumping up and down, running around and doing other vigorous exercise—by burning calories faster, by generating more body heat to keep up with the heat loss.

Well, the situation's exactly the same with our homes. The house "wears" its insulation for the same reason we wear an outer garment in cold weather—to keep heat in. The question is this: What's your house got on? A thin, threadbare sweater or a down-filled parka? If it's wearing that thin sweater, then the house will have to burn more energy to keep warm. And it's a lot cheaper these days to buy the house a down-filled parka than it is to feed the heating system more fuel. For a house, that down-filled parka is added insulation. And the effectiveness of that parka is measured in *R-values*. It's important to understand R-values, because then you'll

*What does your house wear in winter?*

know just how heavy a parka to buy your home. So here's a primer on—

## —R-Values

Imprinted on every batt or blanket of insulation or on every bag of loose insulation is its R-number. The higher the R-number, the more insulation value you're getting and the more money you're saving. (Maybe instead of rating insulating materi. R-3 and R-4 and R-5, it would be more graphic to rate them with dollar signs: $-3, $-4, $-5.)

> The "R" in R-numbers is not just an arbitrary letter. It stands for "resistance"—resistance to heat loss in cold weather; and, in hot weather, resistance to the sun's heat.
> How can insulation work both ways? Because *heat flows naturally to cooler areas.* Thus, in the winter, the heat flows from your nice, warm house to the frigid outdoors, and in the summer the heat flows from outdoors toward your cooler house. Insulation blocks—resists—that flow, helping your house stay warmer in winter and cooler in summer.
> Proper insulation can save your *twenty* to *forty percent* of your home-heating bill in the winter and about ten to fifteen percent of your cost for home cooling in the summer.

How many R's do you need? Well, that all depends on where you live. Find your home-heating zone on the map.

Now, check the chart to see how much insulation you need in your attic floor, exterior wall and other areas.

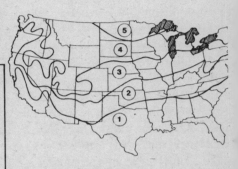

*Heating Zones.*

If your house has no attic (most flat-roof houses don't), chances are there's a cockloft (a space between roof and ceiling at the top-floor level) that can be

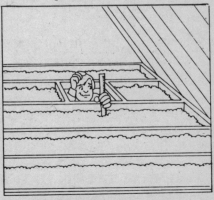

*Measure your present attic insulation with a ruler.*

## RECOMMENDED R-VALUES

| Heating Zone | Attic Floors | Exterior Walls | Ceilings Over Unheated Crawlspace or Basement |
|---|---|---|---|
| 1 | R-26 | R-Value of full wall | R-11 |
| 2 | R-26 | insulation which is | R-13 |
| 3 | R-30 | 3½" thick, will depend | R-19 |
| 4 | R-33 | on material used. | R-22 |
| 5 | R-38 | Range is R-11 to R-13 | R-22 |

insulated. Some cocklofts have hatches that are easily removed. If yours doesn't, remove a ceiling light fixture and check around the edges for insulation. Or, in a closet, poke a hole in the ceiling material and check. (Cocklofts are difficult to insulate. That work should be done by a skilled and reputable professional.)

How do you check to see if your exterior walls (those facing the outside) are insulated? I have four ways:

- Remove a light-switch plate or electrical-outlet plate on an exterior wall and check around the outside edges of the terminal box with a flashlight.

- Go into your basement and look up between the exterior wall's two-by-fours if the framing is open in the basement (you'll find this is the case in unfinished basements).

- Go into a closet against an exterior wall; poke a hole in the wallboard with a screwdriver and examine it with a flashlight.

- Look for "ghosts." On an exterior wall or a ceiling that hasn't been painted for a while, dust particles accumulate in vertical strips between the wall and framing, making a ghostly outline of the studs on the wall (see sketch). This occurs only on uninsulated walls and ceilings.

To see if your floors are insulated, check in basement (if unfinished) or crawlspace. If you've got a finished basement with a ceiling, remove a light fixture and check with a flashlight.

Now that you know where you need insulation, you're ready to go. But wait! What kind of insulation do you need?

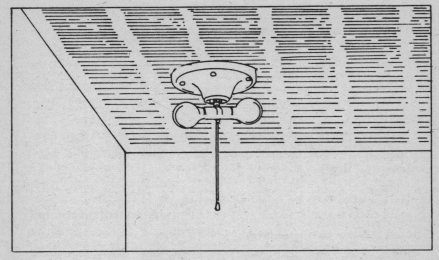

*"Ghosts" on uninsulated ceiling.*

## Types of Insulation

There are three basic types of insulation. All are highly effective, if properly installed. Within each basic type are insulating materials of different characteristics.

---

**THE THREE BASICS ARE:**

1. **Inorganic**—Products made from minerals, such as fiberglass, fibrous stone and vermiculite.
2. **Organic**—Products made from vegetation, such as wood, seaweed and waste-paper products.
3. **Chemical**—Products made from petroleum.

---

There are five ways of applying insulation:

**Batts:** These are rolls of insulation material which are placed within the framing of a structure. Batts are easy to apply—often needing only to be rolled out in your attic space or stapled between the studs of a wall. Almost any do-it-yourselfer can install batts of insulation.

**Blankets:** Similar to batts, blankets come in uniform-cut lengths. They are used in similar areas and, like batts, are easy to handle and present little challenge to most do-it-yourselfers.

**Loose:** These are particles of insulating materials packaged in bags and easily poured between wood frames in your attic. Again, an easy-to-install material for most people. Or, it can be blown into place by professionals.

**Foam:** These are chemicals which are blown or pumped into the area to be insulated. They then solidify, forming a barrier to

*Only a professional should install blown insulation.*

heat loss. Foam insulation can *only* be applied by skilled, trained professionals.

**Boards:** This is insulation material that resembles ceiling tiles. It can be cut with a razor

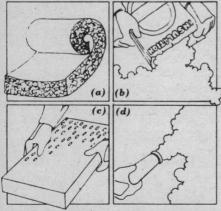

*Four types of insulation: batts (a), loose fill (b), boards (c), foam (d).*

knife or saw, and then nailed, stapled or glued into position.

# CAVEAT EMPTOR

**Before you buy any insulation, read this:**

Different cities, towns, counties and states have different flammability standards. Before you spend your hard-earned money on any insulation, check your local fire and building ordinances to see which types of materials are acceptable in your area.

Beware of insulation that is not wrapped in factory packaging or that bears the names of unfamiliar firms. Some fly-by-night operators are cashing in on the rush to conserve energy by making improperly treated and even dangerous insulation materials and selling them at cut-rate prices. You may pay more for a well-known brand name, but the added cost is an investment in your family's safety and your own peace of mind. Remember, insulation is a one-time investment that pays dividends forever, so don't cut corners and take risks. Insulation should have a label from Underwriters Laboratories, or another recognized testing agency.

And, before installing *any* of the chemical insulation materials, check with your local office of the United States Consumer Product Safety Commission. There have been many reported cases of chemical

## NONORGANIC (MINERAL)

| | Fiberglass Batts & Blankets | Fiberglass loose blown poured | Rock-wool Batts & Blankets | Rock-wool loose blown poured |
|---|---|---|---|---|
| **R VALUE** | | | | |
| R-11 | 3½-4" | 5" | 3" | 4" |
| R-19 | 6-6½" | 8-9" | 5" | 6-7" |
| R-22 | 6¾-7" | 10" | 6" | 7-8" |
| R-30 | 9½-10½" | 13-14" | 9" | 10-11" |
| R-38 | 12-13" | 17-18" | 10½" | 13-14" |
| **Fire Resistant** | Yes | Yes | Yes | Yes |
| **Moisture Resistant** | In some cases | In some cases | No | No |
| **Vermin Proof** | Yes | Yes | Yes | Yes |
| **Rot Proof** | Yes | Yes | Yes | Yes |
| **Corrosive** | No | No | No | No |

insulation materials giving off toxic fumes that have caused eye, nose and throat irritations, and many are highly flammable.

Now that you've graduated from Insulation University, it's time to learn—

## WHERE TO INSULATE

Remember that down-filled parka you were going to put on your house? Well, in considering *where* you need insulation, let's think about the parka again.

| | CHEMICAL | | | | | ORGANIC |
|---|---|---|---|---|---|---|
| Vermiculite loose blown poured | Perlite loose blown poured | Plasticfoam boards | Urethane boards | Ureafoam pumped | | Cellulose fiber loose blown poured |
| 5″ | 4″ | 2¼″ | 1½″ | 2″ | | 3″ |
| 9″ | 7″ | 4¼″ | 2¾″ | 3½″ | | 6″ |
| 10½″ | 8″ | 4½″ | 3″ | 4″ | | 6″ |
| 14″ | 11″ | 6½″ | 4½″ | 5½″ | | 8″ |
| 18″ | 14″ | 8½″ | 5½″ | 7½″ | | 10″ |
| Yes | Yes | No | No | Yes | | No, if not treated |
| In some forms | In some forms | Yes | Yes | Yes | | No |
| Yes | Yes | Yes | Yes | Yes | | No, if treated improperly |
| Yes | Yes | Yes | Yes | Yes | | No, if not treated |
| No | No | No | No | Yes, in some cases | | Yes, if treated improperly |

If you're outside on a cold day with a parka that's a couple of sizes too large for you, you're going to feel colder than if you're wearing one that fits you properly—because a large, loose parka will let cold air in and your body's heat out.

Also, you can have the best-insulated, best-fitting parka in the world, but if you leave the zipper unzipped, it's not going to do you much good.

It's much the same way with your house. You want to keep the insulation close to the *heated*

**19**

areas (you don't want to keep warm air *in* your attic, you want to keep it in the living quarters *beneath* the attic, so you insulate the attic floor, not the attic ceiling), and you don't want to leave "unzipped" gaps through which the warm air will escape (like an uninsulated attic trapdoor).

---

**CAUTION**

Urea Formaldehyde (UF) foam insulation (which is pumped into walls only by contractors) has been installed in half a million American homes. The Consumer Product Safety Commission reports more than 600 consumer complaints about unhealthful effects from formaldehyde gas released by UF foam insulation. The complaints include difficulty in breathing, eye and skin irritations, headaches, dizziness, nausea, vomiting and severe nosebleeds. The commission is also studying possible long-term effects of formaldehyde gas exposure, such as birth defects and links to cancer. UF foam has been banned in some states.

---

The following illustration shows you where insulation should be placed:

## WHERE TO INSULATE

The diagram shows where insulation goes.

Ceilings with cold spaces above.

Exterior walls. The short walls of a split-level house should not be neglected. Walls between living space and unheated garages or storage rooms should be insulated, too. Walls that are enclosed on both sides can be insulated only by an insulation contractor.

Floors above cold spaces— vented crawlspaces, garages, open porches, and any portion of a floor in a room that extends beyond the wall below.

A.   Between attic collar beams.

B.   In cockloft beneath flat roof.

C.   In roof rafters adjacent to living spaces.

D.   Attic floors.

E.   In knee walls adjacent to attic spaces.

F.   In knee walls adjacent to attic crawlspaces.

G.   In exterior walls adjacent to unheated spaces.

H.   In exterior walls.

I.   In sloping roofs over heated areas.

J. Ceilings below unheated areas.

K. Exterior walls below window sections.

L. Floors above crawlspaces.

M. Exposed framing above foundations.

N. Foundation walls in heated basements.

**21**

## IT'S EASY

Don't let the diagram on the preceding page overwhelm you!

There are a lot of places to install insulation, but in almost every case it's an easy job; one requiring minimal mechanical skills.

And, since most insulation is hidden from view, you don't have to install it with a cabinet-maker's precision. Because of this, I find insulating is kind of fun — it's so much less demanding than a lot of other household repair jobs. The chances are good that you've got everything you need for the job around your house, except the insulating material. So you've got no excuse — get on with it and watch those fuel savings pile up!

## VENTILATE YOUR
### Insulated Areas

Well insulated attics, crawlspaces, storage areas and other closed cavities should be well ventilated to prevent excessive moisture build-up.

You know *where* to insulate, but there's still one more thing to know... and that's about—

## —VAPOR BARRIERS

## It Doesn't Rain Inside Your House, But It Does Dew

Walk out on your lawn on a cool summer morning and you'll find the ground wet—not with rain, but with dew.

Pour yourself a glass of ice water in a nice, warm house and you'll find the outside of the glass wet—from dew.

Install insulation without a vapor barrier and dew will form, rotting wood, corroding electrical wiring and eroding plaster.

If it doesn't rain in your house, why should you have dew?

Warm air holds more moisture than cold air. Your breathing adds moisture to the air. Cooking increases the humidity inside the house. And so does a humidifier. When that warm, moisture-laden air hits the cold surfaces in unheated portions of the attic and walls, dew forms. But if you can place something to stop the moisture between the cold surface and the heated air, dew won't form. Unfortunately, insulation won't do that job by itself—in fact, most insulation materials would *collect* the moisture, and wet insulation doesn't work. So you need a vapor barrier between the warm portions of the house and the insulation.

Many batts and blankets of insulation have a vapor barrier already attached. *All you have to remember to do is install the in-*

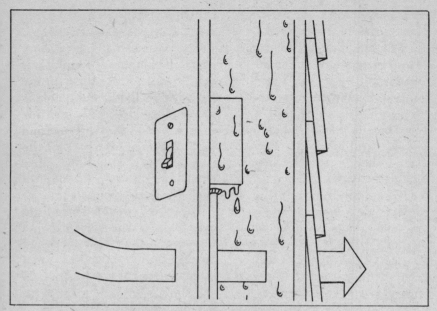

*When there is no vapor barrier, dew forms
when heated interior air hits colder outside air between walls.*

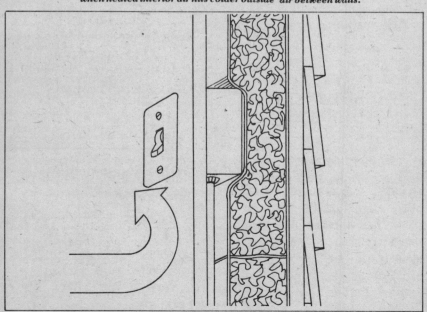

*Vapor barrier blocks moisture in heated air
and keeps it in the house, preventing dew from forming.*

23

sulation with the vapor barrier closest to the heated area (it's not hard to remember, since most vapor barriers have that instruction printed on them). For other forms of insulation, it is necessary to lay down or nail up a vapor barrier (usually aluminum foil, saturated kraft paper or plastic sheeting) before installing the insulation.

Often, when insulating a cockloft or exterior wall, it is impractical or impossible to install a vapor barrier. In those cases, a moisture-blocking effect can be created by papering the wall with a vinyl wallpaper or by painting the wall or ceiling with two coats of good-quality oil-based paint.

Okay, you're ready to begin—

# —INSTALLING INSULATION YOURSELF

**It's so easy you'll feel like a million bucks doing it. And you'll save hundreds.**

How much do you need?

To figure out how many square feet of insulation you'll need, measure in feet the length and width of the area to be covered, multiply the two dimensions and you'll have the square footage of insulation material. Now meas-

ure the distance between the wall studs or joists (those wooden frames). If you're using batts or blankets of insulation, you'll want to buy them in the right widths (batts and blankets are made in 16-, 20-, and 24-inch widths). If you're using a poured insulation material, the bag will tell you how many square feet a bag will cover at each of several R-numbers.

If you're in doubt, buy a little extra to be on the safe side, and be sure you can return unopened bags and still-wrapped batts and blankets.

## Insulating Your Attic:

---

### CAUTION
Watch out for nails protruding through roofing boards. You want a warm house, not a hole in the head. *Don't* step off the floor framing or walking board. You don't want a hole in your ceiling, either.

---

## Tools and Equipment:

Long-sleeved shirt
A  Duct or masking tape, 1½" to 3" wide
B  Hammer
C  Serrated-edge kitchen knife
D  Dust mask
E  Assorted nails

*The tools and equipment you'll need for insulating jobs.*

F  Scissors or shears

G  Gloves

H  Lighting (extension light for those dark corners)

I  Tape measure or ruler

J  Rake (if using loose insulation)

K  Walking board (¾" thick, 16" wide, 4 feet long)

L  Heavy-duty staple gun and staples

You need the long-sleeved shirt, the gloves and the dust mask to protect you from the fibers in the insulation and the dust in the attic. *Never* install insulation without them.

Now, you're ready for an *easy* and rewarding job.

**Starting from scratch:**

If there is no insulation in your attic, roll batts of insulating material between the joists

*Insulating an attic floor with batts. (Be sure you wear that dust mask!)*

(frames) with the vapor barrier down.

Or, place vapor barrier between joists; then pour in loose

*Before installing loose insulation, be sure to staple in a vapor barrier...Then, pour in the insulation and level it off.*

insulating material and level with a rake or straight stick.

## If your attic already has some insulation:

Lay new batts of insulation over existing material, at right angles

to the joists. But be sure to install new insulation that has *no* vapor barriers, or to slash the vapor barriers on the new batts to enable old insulation to "breathe." Install new batts with the slashed barrier down.

And, if your old insulation has a kraft paper covering facing up, cut slashes in that, to enable moisture to escape into the attic.

Whether you're installing the

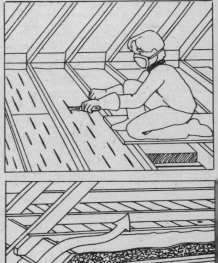

*Your attic must breathe. Don't let insulation block eaves. Air must flow up through eaves and out ventilator openings.*

first insulation in your attic or increasing the insulation already there, be sure you don't block ventilation openings in the eaves and in gable ends.

Don't smoke while working in the attic. The dust could be combustible and cause a fire. (Besides, you're supposed to be wearing a dust mask, and you can't smoke with a dust mask on.)

## Attic Trapdoors

Remember that unzipped down-filled parka? Well, your attic trapdoor can be like that open parka zipper. Don't forget to insulate it. You can staple insulation material directly to it. (Remember to keep the vapor barrier facing the heated area of the house.)

*Don't forget to insulate your attic trapdoor.*

Torn vapor barrier? Don't throw it away, patch it! Use masking tape and fix tears—no matter how small—in vapor barriers.

*Protect protruding lighting fixtures from insulation with a shield made from sheet metal or a coffee can.*

## CAUTION

Don't insulate around lighting fixtures, motors or any other electrical equipment mounted through the attic floor. Keep insulation at least three inches from these objects.

Exercise extreme care in handling electrical cables and wires in the attic or anywhere else you are installing insulation. Rough handling could cause a short circuit or a fire.

## HINT

You can make a frame to keep insulation a safe distance from electrical equipment with sheet metal or a large coffee can.

Some people develop reactions to certain insulating materials — reactions such as skin irritations, burning eyes, sore throats. Check with your doctor if you develop these symptoms.

*Don't forget to insulate under floorboards or catwalks in your attic.*

## Attic Walkways

That flooring over the joists may hide an uninsulated area. Even if you have to temporarily remove the flooring, it's worthwhile to get insulation between those joists. You may be able to squeeze it there by pushing and pulling if the walkway isn't too wide.)

---

**HINT**

Insulate all heating and cooling ductwork in attic, basement or crawlspace with at least two or three inches of fiberglass.

---

*Be sure you insulate around chimneys and pipes in your attic.*

## Attic Pipes

Vent pipes and electrical conduits and chimneys coming up through your attic floor should have insulation hand-packed around them to prevent warm air loss through ceiling cracks.

*Insulate all heating and air-condition ducts in crawlspaces and attics.*

## WHAT WILL IT COST?

Insulating your attic will cost about forty to fifty cents a square foot.

## HOW MUCH WILL I SAVE?

If you start with an uninsulated attic and do all I recommend, you'll probably save yourself *twenty percent* on your home heating bill every year from now on. And it's easier than falling off a log—so do it!

# Insulating an Exterior Wall:

## Finished walls

It is all but impossible for a do-it-yourselfer to insulate a finished exterior wall without tearing off the wallboards. Competent professionals can do this work for you. However, there are some sharp, fly-by-night operators in this industry, and you should exercise extreme caution before engaging anyone to blow insulation into your finished walls.

### ENERGY-SAVING SEATING

Whenever possible, place chairs, couches and beds away from exterior walls. You'll feel less of the outside chill so you won't be pushing that thermostat up to increase your comfort.

## Unfinished walls:

Using blankets the width of your wall studs, insert the blanket between the studs and staple to the studs. (The job is easier if, as in wallpapering, you start from the top and work down.) Be certain the insulation fits snugly against the top piece of framing.

### CAUTION

The vapor barrier must face the *heated* side of the house.

### OR:

Unfinished walls can be insulated using blankets without vapor barriers; a vapor barrier of two-mil-or-more plastic sheeting or foil-backed gypsum board can then be stapled to the studs. (Re-

*Insulating an exposed exterior wall: Staple insulation between studs and then cover with vapor barrier.*

member to keep the plastic taut as you staple it in place.)

You can lose warm air through light-switch plates and wall sockets on exterior (outdoor-facing) walls. Kits are sold in hardware and building supply stores that will remedy the situation. They consist of pre-cut foam insulators that are easily installed under the wall plates.

**Be sure to buy only those kits listed by Underwriters Laboratories (UL).**

It will cost you less than half a dollar per outlet or switch plate and can save you 1.5 percent of your home heating cost.

## Insulating an Unfinished Masonry Wall

You may have unfinished masonry walls in your basement. To insulate them, you've first got to create wall studs to hold the insulation material. Using masonry nails, fasten two-by-two furring strips in place vertically, placing them sixteen or 24 inches apart (measure from the center of each strip to the center of the next strip). Then insulate as with any other unfinished wall.

*Be sure insulation is between pipes and conduits and cold areas, not between them and heated areas.*

### CAUTION

When applying insulation around water pipes, be sure insulating material is between pipes and *outside* wall (the pipes should be *exposed*, not covered). This will keep the pipes from freezing and bursting.

*Insulate openings around window and door frames.*

## Insulating Door and Window Frames

Be sure you get insulation in those spaces around unfinished walls, doors and windows. Since the framing area is narrow, loose insulation must be hand-packed into it.

### WHAT WILL IT COST?

To insulate your exterior walls will cost you about $1 a square foot.

### HOW MUCH WILL I SAVE?

If your exterior walls are uninsulated, installing insulation—or having it installed by a qualified professional—will probably save you *fifteen percent* of your home heating bill every year from now on!

## Insulating the Floor Above a Cold Crawlspace:

For this one you're probably going to have to work flat on your back. But console yourself; that's the way Michelangelo painted the ceiling of the Sistine Chapel.

To begin, drive nails into the floor joists, about eighteen inches apart. This will be used later to "lace" in your insulation.

Now shove batts of insulation up between the joists. They should fit snugly enough to remain there, defying gravity, for a short time. In that period, lace wire back and forth between the nails to fix the insulation permanently in place. Or you can nail chicken wire to the joists to hold the insulation (although that's a bigger job).

**31**

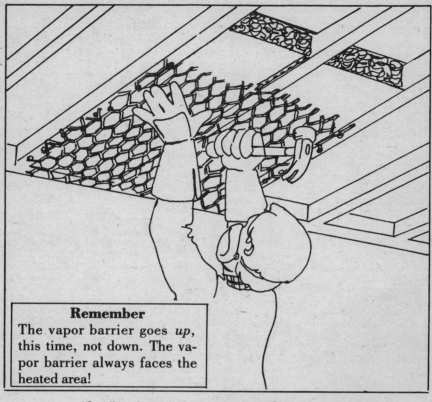

**Remember**

The vapor barrier goes *up*, this time, not down. The vapor barrier always faces the heated area!

*"Lace" insulation in place on crawlspace ceilings with wire.*
*Or nail up chicken wire after you insulate.*

## WHAT WILL IT COST?

Insulating your crawlspace will cost you forty to fifty cents a square foot.

## HOW MUCH WILL I SAVE?

Insulating the floor above a cold crawlspace probably will save you ten percent of your home heating bill. And once you get used to working on your back, it's easy.

*When floor joists are at right angle to the building foundation, nail insulaton to the sill.*

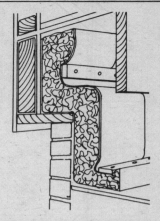

*When floor joist is parallel to the foundation, you'll need a strip of furring to nail the insulation in place.*

### HINT

When insulating a crawl-space, be certain to insulate the rim joist and the floor joists where the subfloor meets the building end. This will close the last open zipper on your home's down-filled parka.

### BUT

Be certain you don't cover foundation vents with insulation.

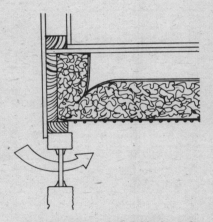

*Be sure insulation doesn't block crawl-space ventilation grilles.*

## Insulating Your Unused Rooms

If you've got a big, old, partially occupied house, you may want to save on your fuel bills by not heating (or air conditioning) unused rooms. But when you begin shutting off radiators, convectors or air vents, remember you'll save even more by putting some insulation between the rooms you shut off and the rooms you're continuing to heat.

You can do that by insulating the interior walls of the room you're shutting off or—as a

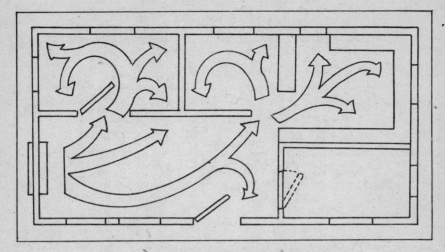

*Block off unused rooms and don't heat them.*

## DON'T FORGET THAT GARAGE

Whether your attached garage is heated or not, it should be sealed up against the winter weather. Weatherstrip and caulk the doors and windows, and insulate the walls that adjoin the living space of the house. (See page 40 on weatherstripping and page 42 on caulking.) Remember to keep the vapor barrier facing the *living areas*, not the garage areas. You might also consider installing a storm door between garage and house. But don't make the garage airtight. **Fumes must be able to escape!**

quick-fix solution—by hanging blankets or quilts on those walls. Also, if you store a lot of furniture, paperwork, merchandise or other non-perishables in the unheated room, their bulk will create insulation and cut down heat loss from the parts of the house you want to keep warm.

Now that the ceiling, walls and crawlspaces are insulated, it's time to turn our attention toward—

## —WINDOWS AND DOORS

Do you know where the word "window" comes from? It's a combination of "wind" and "door," and originally meant a door through which the wind blew—literally, the wind's door.

In this day of expensive home-heating fuels, the last thing you want is for your windows to be doors for the cold wind. You can take steps to significantly cut heat loss through your windows.

You already have a solar heating system, for a window can actually *serve* your heating needs. It can act as a conduit for the sun's energy and let in radiant heat faster than it lets out your furnace-created heat. This is the simplest form of solar energy—a form we can *all* take advantage of, without expensive solar collectors or heat distribution systems. It's called "passive" solar heating.

In general, south-facing windows admit the most heat, followed by east, then west exposures. Since north-facing windows admit little or no heat and tend to conduct room heat out of the house, you can fight that effect by keeping blinds, curtains or shutters drawn on those windows. (And remember to do the same for your heat-collecting windows during the *night*, too.)

That solar collector window of yours has got to collect more heat than it loses. Unfortunately, a lot of windows let out more heat than they take in. In fact, in the average house, each improperly insulated window will waste about one percent of your home-heating dollars. Properly in-

## CLEAN THAT GLASS

Your passive solar collector (your window) works better clean than dirty. Dirt on the window panes absorbs the sun's rays and doesn't let the heat in. Keep those south-, east- and west-facing windows clean, (and while you're at it, you might as well clean the north windows too). A fringe benefit: More sunlight means a brighter room, which means you don't have to turn on your lights as much, saving you money on your electric bill.

sulating ten windows can save you ten percent of your fuel costs.

You can save a lot of money using storm windows, but, if the primary windows are in poor condition, your storm windows won't be as effective. So the first step is:

## INSPECT YOUR WINDOWS

Check to see if your windows *are* open doors for the wind. Look for:

- Broken or cracked glass
- Broken, loose or missing latches
- Loose sashes and frames

**35**

*Inspect windows for broken glass, broken latches, missing caulking and putty.*

- Cracked or missing putty around panes or damaged weatherstripping
- Lack of weatherstripping
- Lack of caulking

**CAUTION**

Many pamphlets and books — including some from government agencies — advise testing for air leaks around windows by moving a lighted candle around the frame to see if it flickers. That test can be dangerous. The candle can ignite curtains or draperies. I advise moving a single sheet of dangling tissue paper around the frame. If the tissue is blown away from the window or sucked toward it, you've got an air leak that's costing you money.

Here's how to fix each possible window problem:

**Broken Window Pane**

To fix a broken window pane, you'll need:

| | |
|---|---|
| Gloves | Large piece of |
| Cornstarch | cardboard |
| Putty knife | Can of putty |
| Pliers | Box of glazier's |
| Scissors | points |
| Paintbrush | Boiled linseed |
| Electric iron or | oil |
| propane torch | |

Remove all the old broken glass from the frame. (Be sure to wear gloves to protect your hands from the jagged edges.) Now, using the propane torch, heat up the old putty and remove it with the putty knife and pliers. (You can use an electric iron to heat the putty if you don't have a propane torch and don't want to buy one.)

Using the pliers, carefully pull out the old glazier's points (those are the little metal triangles or staples that hold the glass in place). Cut your cardboard to fit the window frame, then trim 1/8″ from the top and from *one* side of the cardboard (this creates a 1/16″ margin on each of the cardboard's four sides). Now have a glazier or hardware store cut a piece of window glass to the exact size of the cardboard.

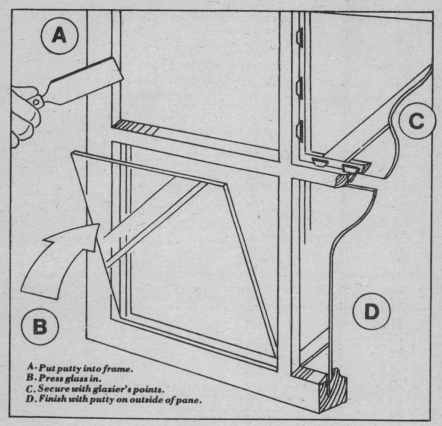

A. Put putty into frame.
B. Press glass in.
C. Secure with glazier's points.
D. Finish with putty on outside of pane.

Returning to your window, sprinkle cornstarch on your hands and on any surface where you'll be rolling putty. This keeps the putty from sticking where you don't want it.

Next, roll all the putty in the can into a 3/8″ to 1/2″ diameter rope. Brush a light coat of linseed oil onto the frame and press the putty rope into the oiled frame (cut the putty rope into six-inch lengths for easier handling). Now, press the glass into the frame and remove all but 1/16″ of putty squeezed out by the pressure of the glass.

Wedge the glazier's points into the frame with the blade of the putty knife, spacing them about eight inches apart. Then cut the remainder of your putty rope into six-inch lengths and squeeze into the corner of the window frame. Smooth and remove the excess putty with the putty knife, and you've sealed a window and saved some heating dollars.

## Broken, Loose or Missing Window Latches

That window latch is there for more than security — it presses the top and bottom sash together to eliminate outside air infiltration or inside heat loss. If the latch is broken, loose or missing, you're losing heating dollars. To install a new latch you'll need:

New latch    Center punch
Hammer      or awl
Ruler        Wood screws
Petroleum   Cake of soft
   jelly        soap

First remove the old, broken or loose latch, then close the window tightly. Measure and mark the center of the joined sash frames. Place the turning latch section of the lock on the center mark at the top of the lower sash frame. With a hammer and awl, punch guide holes through the screw ports on the turning latch section. Lubricate wood screws by rubbing them over the bar of soap and then screw the turning latch section firmly into position. Now line up the hook section on the bottom of the frame of the upper sash, making sure it is even with the turning latch section. Punch holes as you did for the first part of the latch, soap and drive screws into place and lubricate your new latch with petroleum jelly.

*Window latches keep sashes firmly closed against the cold.*

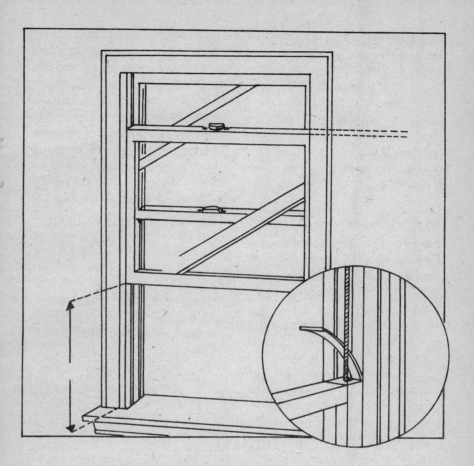

*A strip of linoleum in the window channel can tighten loose sashes.*

## Loose Sashes

You usually know if your sashes are loose because they tell you— by rattling when the wind blows. That rattle means cold air's coming in and warm air's going out. To fix a loose sash, you'll need:

Piece of          Shears
    linoleum      Paraffin wax or
Carpet tacks          silicone spray
Small hammer   Ruler

If your lower sash is loose, raise it and measure the opening, then add six inches. Next measure the thickness of the sash and subtract 1/8". Cut strips of linoleum to those measurements and slip one into the sash groove (if your window has metal weatherstripping, you must slip the linoleum under the weatherstripping). Tack the linoleum in place and close the window. Now tack the six-inch section of linoleum above the top of the sash frame. If the sash still rattles, add more linoleum strips. Lubricate the linoleum strips with the paraffin wax or silicone spray. If it is the top sash that's loose, lower it and repeat the measuring and linoleum-strip installation process.

## Loose Frames

As a house ages, entire window frames work themselves loose because nails corrode and wood rots. To fix loose frames, you'll need:

Hammer

Screwdriver

Screws and/or nails at least 3" long

Oakum (hemp saturated with linseed oil — available in larger hardware stores or plumbing supply stores)

Caulking gun

Caulking compound

Framing square

Wood shingles

Check the frame to see if it is square. If not, the window won't operate properly. To square up a frame, wedge wooden shingles in around the sides of the frame between it and the house frame (you may have to remove some molding to do this). When the window is square, drive nails or screws through the window frame and shingle wedges into the house frame. Using the saw, cut off the excess shingle material as close

to the frame as possible.

After the frame is solid, stuff oakum into all spaces around the entire window. This will insulate the spaces and provide a support for the caulking material. Next caulk around the entire window frame and replace any molding you may have removed.

## Lack of Weatherstripping

Weatherstripping is insulating material in thin strips designed to block heat loss through narrow window sash cracks and through the spaces around the edges of doors. You can get weatherstripping in several forms — spring metal weatherstripping is the longest-lasting, but the most difficult to install. Adhesive-backed foam-rubber weatherstripping and adhesive-backed felt strips are easy to install, but wear quickly. Rolled vinyl

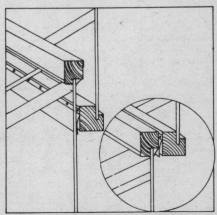

*Spring metal weatherstripping on window rails.*

**40**

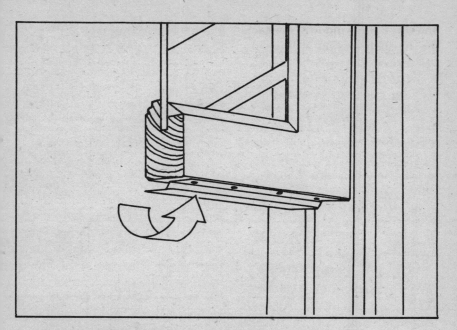

*Spring metal weatherstripping on window frame bottom*

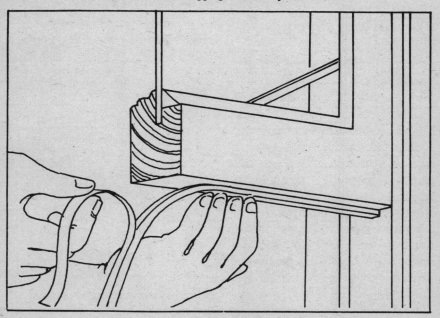

*Pressure-sensitive weatherstripping on window frame bottom*

**41**

weatherstripping is longer-lasting than foam rubber or felt and is as easy to install.

Measure your windows and buy the appropriate amount of weatherstripping. Remember to install weatherstripping along the sashes and the sash frame tops and bottoms. Carefully follow the manufacturer's instructions with whatever type of weatherstripping you buy for most effective insulation.

---

**WHAT WILL IT COST?**

Weatherstripping all doors and windows in an average one-family house should cost about $30.

**HOW MUCH WILL I SAVE?**

A good, tight-fitting job of weatherstripping on all doors and windows will probably save you ten percent of your home heating bill every year from now on!

---

**HINT**

Check your weatherstripping every year. Weatherstripping wears out faster than most other insulation, and needs to be replaced to maintain fuel savings.

---

## Lack of Caulking

Caulking seals your house's seams against heat loss. In addition to caulking around window frames, you should caulk wherever two different materials or parts of the house join. So, as long as you're going to buy a caulking cartridge, you also ought to check the area where the chimney and roof shingles meet, between roof dormers and shingles, all roof flashing, the undersides of eaves and gable moldings, between masonry steps and the main structure of the house, at corners formed by siding and between siding panels and any protrusions from the main structure of the house such as hose connections, outside electrical panel boxes and ventilators.

---

**HOW MUCH CAULKING COMPOUND DO I NEED?**

About half a cartridge per window.

About half a cartridge per door.

About two cartridges per chimney.

About four cartridges for the foundation sill.

---

*Where to caulk.*

To do any caulking, you'll need:

Chisel
Wire Brush
Heating pad
Old rags
Oakum or
  fiberglass
Pocket knife
Naphtha

Medium flat
  screwdriver
Cartridge
  caulking gun
Cartridges of
  caulking
  compound

Before you begin, warm the caulking cartridges in a heating pad to make the compound easier to apply. Inspect the area to be caulked and clean off old paint, dirt, deteriorated caulk, using naphtha and a putty knife or screwdriver.

Place the caulking cartridge

**Before buying any caulking compound cartridges, consult the chart below to determine which is best for your purposes:**

## CAULKING CHART

| | Latex | Vegetable oil | Silicone |
|---|---|---|---|
| **Tack-free time** | 15-35 min. | 2-26 hours | 60 min. |
| **Ease of use** | good | fairly good | fairly good |
| **Longevity** | 10 years | 5 years | 20 years |
| **Application temperature** | 40°F | 60°F | 5°F |
| **Adhesion to:** | | | |
| **Wood** | excellent | fairly good. | excellent |
| **Metal** | poor | fairly good | excellent |
| **Painted surface** | excellent | fairly good | excellent |
| **Masonry** | good | fairly good | very good |

in the gun. Using the pocket knife, cut the tip off the cartridge at a 45° angle and insert the screwdriver to break the seal inside the cartridge. Then pull the gun's trigger and squeeze out the compound, *pushing*, not pulling, the gun into the frame of the window. Drawing a good bead of caulk may take a little practice, but you'll get the hang of it. A good bead, incidentally, *overlaps* both sides of the crack for a tight seal.

Fill in cracks that are too wide for a caulking compound bead with oakum or fiberglass and finish the job with caulk.

| Butyl | Nitrile | Acrylic polymeric | Polysulfide |
|---|---|---|---|
| 30-90 min. | 10-25 min. | 10-30 min. | 24-72 hours |
| fairly good | fairly good | poor | fairly good |
| 20 years | 20 years | 20 years | 20 years |
| 40°F | 35°F | warm to 120°F | 5°F |
| excellent unpainted | excellent unpainted | very good | excellent if primed |
| excellent unpainted | excellent unpainted | very good | excellent |
| fair | fair | very good | do not use |
| excellent unpainted | excellent unpainted | very good | excellent if primed |

## WHAT WILL IT COST?

A caulking gun costs about $2. The cartridges can cost up to $4 each. Using the most expensive caulking material, it shouldn't cost you more than $100 to caulk all open cracks around your windows and other spots.

## HOW MUCH WILL I SAVE?

A well-caulked house will cost about ten percent less to heat.

## HINT

Caulking wears out eventually. Check caulked areas every year and recaulk where needed.

## CAUTION

Lead-base caulk is toxic. Some states ban its sale and use. Avoid it.

## CAUTION

If you have to use a ladder to caulk your windows and roof areas, be sure the ladder is level and block it in place. Have someone hold it steady if possible. Get down and move the ladder—*don't* stretch out for hard-to-reach spots. Make a sling for your caulking gun, so you can use both hands climbing the ladder.

## PAINT THAT CAULK

A coat of paint over your caulking compound will seal it against the wind. (Besides, it'll look better.)

## WHAT A WASTE!

**Half** the fuel used in the average American residence for heating is **wasted!** That's right, fifty percent of that warm air the average furnace is making slips outside through cracks, leaks and inadequately insulated roofs and walls.

### Shades, Blinds and Drapes

Shades, blinds, drapes and shutters can save you heating dollars, if you use the right types at the right times.

Earlier, when I was discussing passive solar energy, I talked about keeping shades or drapes drawn on northern exposures since there isn't much sunlight to be received through them and they tend to conduct heat *out* of the house.

At night, when there's no sunlight to gather, you're best off shutting all the drapes, shutters or blinds to create that extra layer of material over the windows and minimize heat loss. (In

*Make sure drapes cover entire window.*

summertime, to maximize cooling and to save energy on air conditioning, simply reverse the procedure—open the shades, windows, shutters, etc. at night to let in the cooler night air and button them up in the daytime, to keep out the sun's radiant energy.)

**What kinds of shades?** Naturally, the tighter the weave of your drapes, the better they'll work as insulation. Lined drapes are more effective than unlined. Roll shades, if pulled all the way down, are more effective than venetian blinds.

And a good, tight fit is important, too. Make sure those shades and drapes leave virtually no space for warm air to escape at the sides, top or bottom.

**47**

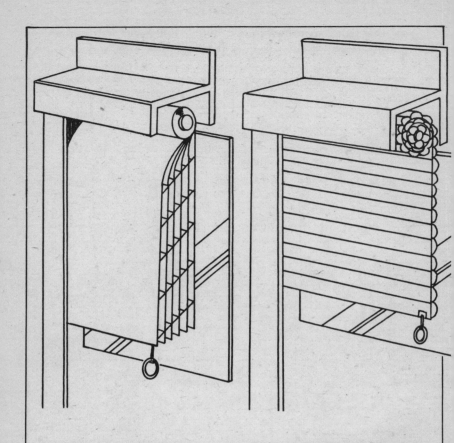

*Multiple-layer insulating window shade.*  *Dead air space insulation window shade.*

## INSULATED SHADES

There are two basic types of insulated shades on the market. Both are mounted in tracks along the sides of the window to eliminate air leaks at the edges. One type has a high R-value and is formed of multiple layers of plastic film. When drawn, the layers of film in the shades create multiple dead air spaces. A second type resembles vene-tian blinds when drawn, but the slats are actually rounded on the window side to create dead air spaces. Unlike blinds, however, the slats are connected by flexible joints. The dead air space in each slat, plus the dead air space between the slats and the window give the shade its insulating properties. To let in light, the slats roll up into a valance above the window.

Now that your windows and doors are straight, tight, clean, caulked and weatherstripped, it's time to consider a final step in equipping them to save you fuel dollars—

# —STORM WINDOWS AND DOORS

Storm windows and doors work by creating a pocket of dead air between the primary window or door and the outside. The dead air acts as insulation, preventing heat loss or cold air infiltration.

Dozens of manufacturers turn out a bewildering number of storm window models. It's easy to become confused and just buy by price. But the cheapest isn't necessarily the best bargain, and the most expensive doesn't necessarily assure you top quality. Storm windows and doors must be carefully chosen and carefully installed. An improperly designed or poorly fitted storm window won't give you anywhere near the heat savings you're paying for.

When buying storm windows, check them for strength and appearance. The corners should be airtight and strong. They should have "weep holes"—tiny vents or drains which allow water condensation to escape from the dead air space. Without weep holes, the water will collect on your window sills and rot them. Check the hardware—it must be as well-made and sturdy as the rest of the window.

Be certain the storm windows you select have permanent weatherstripping or a vinyl gasket to seal the crack between them and the primary windows.

And remember, anodized- or baked-enamel-finish windows will look better longer. Bare aluminum windows will deteriorate faster and become quite unpleasant to handle as oxidation pits and mars them.

Shop around and shop carefully. Take your time. You're making a big investment and you don't want it to turn into a big mistake. Storm windows and doors can pay bigger dividends if you're a careful consumer.

There are two basic kinds of storm windows available—and a third, temporary type you can make for yourself at very, very low cost. The basic types of "store-bought" storm windows are *single-pane* or *single-sash* windows and *combination* windows.

## Single-Pane Storm Windows

These windows are a single pane of glass, usually in an aluminum frame, made to measure for your windows. They are fairly easy to install yourself, although you will have to work from a ladder if your house has more than one story or if you've got high primary windows. They can also be installed from the inside.

Some hardware and building supply stores sell kits so you can make your own single-pane windows, if you've got the time and ability. Or, you can order them made for you. Remember, either way, accurate measurements are critical. And just because you've measured one window, don't think you've measured every other window in your house that looks like it. Windows do vary in size. And, in fact, many vary in measurements from top to bottom, so measure all sides of all windows.

---

**HINT**

Save yourself a lot of confusion later on. Number each window on your house and list each window's measurements according to its number. Then number the storm windows when you get them. Installing them will be a matter of matching numbers, rather than a hit-or-miss proposition, trying to match various storm windows to various primary window frames until you get the right ones lined up.

---

Take your measurements to your building supply or hardware store, and be sure the salesperson copies them accurately when ordering your storm windows. Keep a copy of the measurements, and compare your copy with the delivered storm windows to be sure they're right.

Mounting hardware varies from company to company, so follow the manufacturer's directions carefully if you're mounting your single-pane storm windows yourself.

Single-pane storm windows are less expensive than combination windows, but they have one major disadvantage: They must be removed every summer. You get greater convenience—at a greater price—from combination windows.

**Combination Storm Windows**

These windows combine two features—insulation for the winter and screens for the warmer months. They are permanently installed over your primary windows and the storm windows can be opened anytime for cleaning or ventilation.

If you're really handy, you can install the combination windows yourself, but they are more difficult to put up than the single-pane windows.

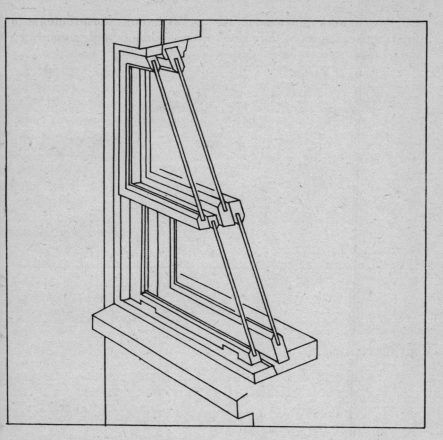

*Combination storm windows combine glass for winter and screens for summer.*

## Plastic Sheeting Storm Windows:

If you don't want to spend $50-$75 per window, there is a temporary storm window you can easily make for yourself. Plastic sheeting storm windows are easy to install and very inexpensive. They are not very attractive, but they are effective insulation and can be taken down anytime. (In fact, you'll have to take them down when the heating season ends.)

The plastic sheeting can be taped up inside your house over existing windows (so you don't

**51**

have to work outdoors and can install them even on the coldest day) or tacked up outside your primary windows.

To do the job you'll need six-mil-thick polyethylene plastic (that's the thick stuff sold in rolls, not the food wrap or the board-like sheets), scissors to cut the plastic, a ruler or yardstick and double-faced adhesive tape or (if you're working outside the house) a hammer, tacks and thin wood strips.

If you are installing the plastic inside the house, measure and cut the plastic to size, cover the four sides of the window frame with the double-faced tape, remove the tape backing from the top, line up the plastic and press in place, remove the rest of the tape backing and smooth the plastic into place.

When installing from the outside, cut the plastic to size, tack to the top of the window frame, using the wood strips to hold the plastic in place; repeat on the sides and bottom.

*Make-it-yourself plastic storm windows are easy and inexpensive, but effective.*

## WRAP IT IN PLASTIC

You can put temporary plastic storm windows over openings already protected by regular aluminum-and-glass storm windows. They'll fight heat loss even more. A good tip for northern exposures subject to strong winds.

## WHAT WILL IT COST?

Prices of storm windows vary widely, running anywhere from $25 to $70 per window. For under $50 you ought to be able to make your own temporary plastic storm windows for your entire house.

## HOW MUCH WILL I SAVE?

You should be able to cut your heating bill by 20 percent with well-fitting storm windows.

## Storm Doors

Storm doors should be inspected the same way storm windows are, and the same considerations about weatherstripping, strong construction and plain or treated aluminum apply. Storm doors are also available with steel and wood frames.

## HINT

Be sure any storm door you buy has safety glass or clear plastic. That door will see a lot of opening, closing and rough treatment from the wind. You don't want the glass shattering in the middle of winter.

More often than not, you'll want a contractor to hang your storm doors. Before you let him slip away, check the fit and the ease of opening and closing. It's much easier to get him to adjust it while he's still there than it is to get him to return to fix things.

## IF YOU MUST MAKE A CHOICE

If you don't want to buy both storm windows and storm doors, bear this in mind: The windows will save you more than the doors. They fit tighter and can be left closed all winter long.

## KEEP IT CLEAN

Storm windows reduce the passive solar heat collecting ability of your windows because the rays have an extra layer of glass to penetrate. So keep those storm windows clean, too, to maximize that free heat from the sun.

## WHICH WINDOWS?

You don't want to lay out that much cash this year? Well, you don't have to do all your windows at once. If you want the most effect for the least expense, do your north-facing windows this year. Next season cover the west-facing windows. Then the east. Leave the southerly exposures for last.

## CHECK THOSE OLD STORM WINDOWS

You already have storm windows? Good! You've had 'em for years? Good! Or is it? Check them. Old storm windows spring air leaks. Check to see that the screws holding them are still tight. And check to see if the aluminum has been buckled by the wind, creating gaps between glass and frame. Caulk gaps from the inside with a clear silicone caulking cartridge.

## HINT

If you've already got storm windows, check to see the weep holes are clean and open. If you've got older storm windows without weep holes, you can make your own with your electric drill.

## Doors

Doors present the same heat-loss problems as windows, but, unless they're the rare, all-glass type, they don't offer the passive solar heat collection opportunities of windows.

Windows can be kept closed all winter, but doors can't—unless you're planning to hibernate.

## SHUT THAT DOOR!

It may sound silly, but the first "door" rule of heat conservation is, "Shut the door." A door swung closed and not latched is going to let a king's ransom in heat out into the cold winter air. So shut the door—and teach your children to shut the door, too.

The best energy-saving door is a revolving door. But homes don't have revolving doors, so you've got to make do with what you do have.

If you've got a vestibule, use it as a cold-air lock. Close the vestibule door behind you before you open the front door. Also, turn off or remove the radiator or heat register in the vestibule. Use the area as a dead air space. Weatherstrip both the vestibule door and the front door and insulate the interior walls of the vestibule.

## Weatherstripping Doors

Almost anyone can weatherstrip a door—they're even easier to do than windows. But there are differences. The top and two sides of a door are frame stripped, while the door bottom requires special treatment.

Each type of weatherstripping is applied in a different manner.

### Pressure-Sensitive Foam Weatherstripping

This weatherstripping comes in rolls with adhesive on one side and an insulating foam on the other. It can be cut with a knife

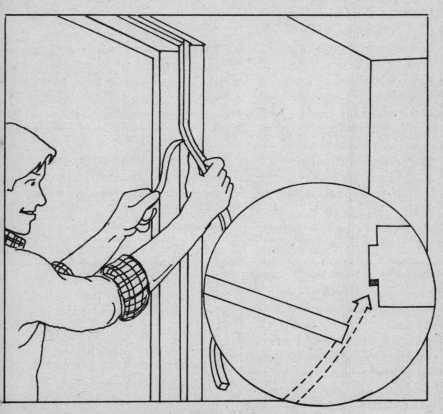

*Pressure-sensitive weatherstripping.*

or scissors and is installed simply by removing the protective backing from the pressure-sensitive adhesive and pressing it against the inside face of the door jamb. (Be sure to wash the jamb first to remove all dirt and grease.)

This type of weatherstripping is extremely easy to install, but it doesn't last very long.

**HINT**

You can reinforce the adhesive's sticking power by putting in a carpet or thumbtack every ten inches or so along the length of the weatherstripping.

*Spring metal weatherstripping.*

*Foam rubber weatherstripping with wood backing.*

## Spring Metal Weatherstripping

This material is easy to install, but, unlike the pressure-sensitive foam, it lasts a long time. You'll need tin snips, hammer, nails and tape measure to do this job. Measure door top and sides, cut strips in length, tack in place along door jamb. For a better seal, lift the outer edge of the strip with a screwdriver after tacking it in place.

## Foam-Rubber Weatherstripping with Wood Backing

This type of weatherstripping comes in rigid strips and must be cut with a hand saw and installed with a hammer and nails. It is easy to install, but doesn't last very long. As with the spring metal weatherstripping, it is cut to length and nailed against the door jamb. Nails should be no more than a foot apart.

*Aluminum-backed vinyl roll weatherstripping.*

## Aluminum-backed vinyl roll weatherstripping

This material consists of a vinyl roll held rigid by an aluminum strip which is nailed to the door jamb. It is easy to install and long-lasting. It's installed the same way as the two previous samples.

| HINT |
|---|
| Keep your weatherstripping clean. It'll last longer and be more effective. |

## Door Bottoms—Sweeps:

Sweeps are brush-like strips that are attached to the bottoms of doors to keep heat inside. They may be vinyl or nylon with either aluminum or plastic backing for rigidity and installation. They work only on flat thresholds and can become snagged on carpets or rugs. They are extremely easy to install, since the door can be left on during installation. Simply cut to proper length and

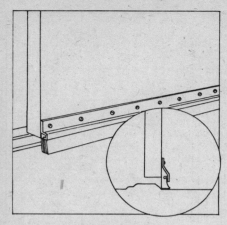

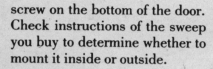

*A door bottom sweep.*

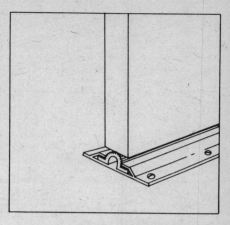

*A door bottom bulb threshold.*

screw on the bottom of the door. Check instructions of the sweep you buy to determine whether to mount it inside or outside.

### Door Bottoms—Shoes, Bulb Thresholds and Interlocking Thresholds

These devices require removing the door and trimming the bottom to make room for the weatherstripping. While a do-it-yourselfer with good skills can install the first two, only a professional carpenter should attempt the interlocking threshold.

Now that you've insulated your door, step out and see what improvements you can make—

> While you're at it, weatherstripping all those doors and windows, don't forget the attic door. A lot of heat can slip through the attic door cracks.

## OUTSIDE YOUR HOUSE—ROOFING AND SIDING

If you're about to re-roof or re-side your house, now's a good time to make some decisions that will save you heating dollars in years to come.

In the colder climates, choose darker-color roofing shingles. The dark shingles will absorb the sun's heat and act as solar collectors. In the hotter, southern areas of the Sunbelt, where cooling is a big consideration, go for lighter colors, which will reflect the sun's heat away from your roof.

In any area, if you're putting on new siding, it will pay you to look for metal or synthetic siding materials with insulation backing. And, when the old siding's

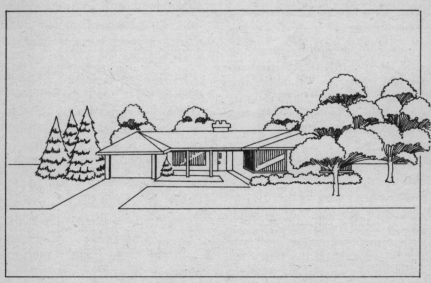

*Ideal landscaping protects the house from the wind but allows in sunlight in winter, shades in the summer.*

off the house, it's a perfect time to insulate those exterior walls or add to the insulation already on them.

## LANDSCAPING

If you were starting from scratch, here's the ideal way to landscape your property for maximum fuel savings: On the northwest side of the house—where the winds usually come from—plant evergreen trees. They will act as windscreens and complement your exterior wall insulation. On all other sides, plant deciduous (leaf-bearing) trees. In winter, when the leaves are off, the sun will be able to penetrate to your roof, warming your home. And in summer, the leaves will shade your roof. Around the house, close to the foundation, plant hedges or other dense bushes.

If you're in a rural area, you may want to buy some hay bales and make a small mound of hay around the house at the foundation. The hay will keep the wind from the house.

If a portion of your home's foundation is exposed to the elements, you may want to consider regrading around your house to cover that portion.

Let's go back inside now and ask—

## HOW ABOUT A GREENHOUSE?

You can supplement your furnace with the sun's energy by installing a greenhouse attached to your house. On sunny days, the greenhouse will collect the sun's heat and a simple fan arrangement can pump that warmth into your home. On cloudy days and at night, close off the greenhouse with storm doors to cut heat loss. Depending on the size, greenhouses cost between $1,500 and $6,000. But they can reduce your home heating bill by as much as 25 percent!

*A greenhouse can be a passive solar heating unit.*

**61**

# —HOW DO YOU HEAT?

What kind of heating system do you have? If you answered "gas," or "oil" or "electricity" or "propane," then you only gave half an answer. What you named was your fuel. What you left out was your actual system. Basically, there are three types of heating systems: *radiant, convection* and *exchange.* Some systems combine radiant and convection. Those aren't necessarily very sophisticated—cavemen heated by a radiant system: They burned logs in the middle of their caves. (In addition to being unsophisticated, it was frequently dangerous because of the deadly gases given off by those burning logs. It makes you wonder how man survived.)

That fireplace of yours supplies radiant heat. The fuel—wood—burns, and what heat is reflected off the fire penetrates the room and, if you sit close enough, warms you. Pretty, but not very efficient.

The ancient Romans went a step further. They used convection systems. They built big fires

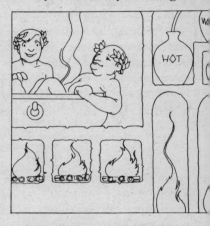

*The Romans used a combination of convection and radiant heat in their ancient baths.*

*Cavepersons used radiant heat only.*

in their basements and detoured the flue pipes through the floors of their houses. Thus, the floors radiated heat to warm the rooms (maybe that's why men, as well as women, wore dress-like garments in those days—to let the heat rise up their legs).

After the Romans, in the dark ages, Europeans went back to radiant heat from fireplaces— and in ancient castles you'll find walk-in size fireplaces in almost every room. You can imagine whole forests going up in smoke while knights and their ladies stood practically inside those giant fireplaces, only to freeze a dozen paces from the hearth.

Later on came steam heat. Wood or coal—and later oil and gas—were burned to heat water to its gasification point (steam is gasified water) and the steam was piped around a building and, through radiators and pipes, gave off heat. This was a combined radiant and convection system.

However, water has to be heated to more than 212 degrees Fahrenheit to turn it into steam. Another radiant and convection system is hot-water heat. Here the water is heated to about 175 degrees and piped around a house. It is quieter than steam and the heating system is simpler.

Forced-air heat, the most common form in this country, is generally an exchange and convection system. The exchange is heated air taking the place of the cold room air. The cold air is extracted and ducted to the furnace for heating.

Why am I telling you all this? So you'll understand how your system works and understand why any obstruction to the proper functioning of the system will make the furnace work longer and cost you money.

Furnaces are generally sophisticated pieces of equipment. Heating systems are delicately balanced interconnections. You may be wary of tackling your system yourself. Well, you're right, for the most part. The big jobs aren't for home handypeople. But there are a few steps you can take to make your system work better. And the rest has to be done for you.

The first and easiest thing to do is to—

## —TURN DOWN THAT THERMOSTAT

The thermostat is the brain of your heating system. The thermostat—a temperature-sensing device somewhere in the living area—turns the furnace on when the temperature in your house drops below a certain point and turns it off again when a previously selected level of warmth is achieved.

If you're used to setting your thermostat at 72°, you can easily learn to live with a lower temperature of 70° or even 68°. (Public buildings are required to set their thermostats no higher than 65° in the winter.)

---

## DRESS RIGHT
In winter, wear a sweater indoors. You'll feel comfortable at lower temperatures.

---

At night, when you're under the covers, you can drop the temperatures even further. Now there's an old myth around that says it doesn't pay to lower the thermostat at night because it takes extra energy to warm the building up to daytime temperatures. *That's not true.* Turning down that thermostat at night will save you anywhere from ten to fifteen percent on your heating costs.

---

## WHAT DOES IT COST?
Nothing.

## HOW MUCH WILL I SAVE?
Depending on your location in the country, you can save as much as twenty percent of your heating fuel bill by lowering your thermostat.

---

Perhaps you want a gadget that will lower your thermostat automatically at night and turn it back up just before you're going

---

**FOR EVERY DEGREE YOU LOWER YOUR THERMOSTAT IN THE WINTER, YOU WILL SAVE ABOUT TWO TO THREE PERCENT IN HEATING COSTS!** A drop of four degrees will save you eight to twelve percent. A drop of five degrees, ten to fifteen percent.

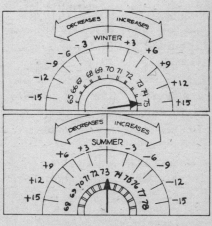

*Percentage of savings (or extra cost) by thermostat degree setting.*

to get out of bed in the morning. There are such devices, called "setbacks." If there's no one home during the day, you may want to buy a "double setback" that will lower the temperature at night, raise it in the morning, lower it again after everyone has left the house for the day, raise it just before the family returns home and dip it again at bedtime.

## HEATED GARAGE?

Turn off the heat in your garage. Your car's comfort isn't worth the price you're paying.

Depending on the level of sophistication, setback devices can cost you anywhere from $65 to $125. Most of them must be installed by professionals although a few are simple enough for a competent do-it-yourselfer.

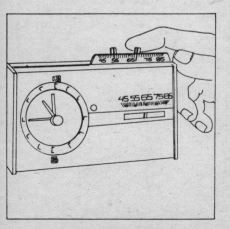

*Lower your thermostat.*

## A WORD OF WARNING—

People *can* live in a house with lowered temperatures and get quite used to it. But it is important to remember that in some cases there are *medical* reasons *not* to turn that thermostat down.

Older people, particularly, are susceptible to *hypothermia*, a sharp drop in body temperature, which can be fatal.

People who have poor circulation or a history of hypothermia and those taking certain families of prescription drugs should take extreme caution not to let the temperature in their homes get too cold.

So, if you fit the category— or have someone living with you who does—don't lower that thermostat unless you first consult a physician.

## WHERE'S YOUR THERMOSTAT?

If your thermostat is on an exterior wall or in a direct line with a door, it is needlessly costing you money. A thermostat should be on an interior wall, away from doors, windows and heating units so it is not affected by drafts from open doors or by air leaks through window cracks or faults in exterior wall insulation. If it's in the wrong place, have it moved. (It's not a job for a do-it-yourselfer.)

## PLUG IN

An electric blanket can keep you comfortable in a cooler room. Turn down your thermostat, turn up your electric blanket. It costs less to heat a bed (even electrically) than to heat a whole house.

## USE A HUMIDIFIER

All summer long, you complained, "It's not the heat that bothers me, it's the humidity." Now here I am telling you that you need a humidifier in your home in the winter months.

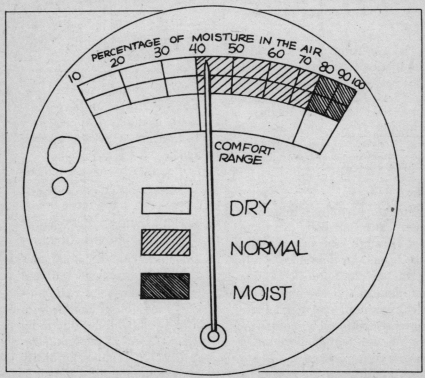

*A hygrometer.*

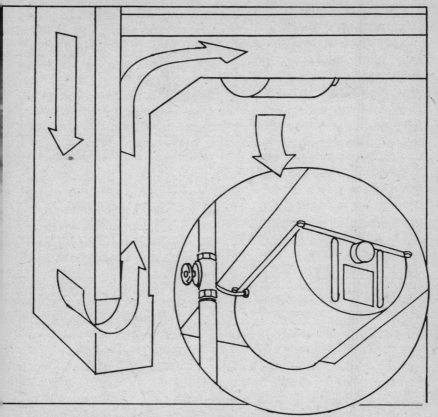

*Built-in humidifier in a forced-air system adds moisture to heated, dry air.*

**Why?**

Moist or humid air holds heat better. And your body loses less heat through evaporation into more humid air than it loses into dry air. So the humid condition that makes you less comfortable in the summer can help make you more comfortable in the winter. You can feel comfortable at lower temperatures if there's more humidity in the air—so a humidifier will help you turn

down that thermostat and save fuel.

Before you buy any humidifier, go out and get yourself a hygrometer. This is a simple device that hangs on your wall and tells you a room's relative humidity. For maximum comfort you want the relative humidity to be between 45 and 75 percent. (The "relative" in relative humidity refers to temperature. Cold air is capable of holding less moisture than warm air. A figure like fifty percent relative humidity means the air has fifty percent of the humidity it can contain *at that temperature*. At 100 percent relative humidity, it's raining—a condition you want to avoid in your home unless you're a duck.)

Once you have your hygrometer, you're capable of adjusting a humidifier to the proper comfort levels.

Some forced-air heating systems have built-in humidifiers. If the one that came with your house is operating properly, you don't need portable units. If you have a forced-air system without a built-in humidifier, it's possible to add one, but that is a job for a professional. Instead—or if you have a hot-water or steam system—you can buy portable units in most hardware, housewares and department stores.

---

## WHAT WILL IT COST?

A built-in humidifier can cost you as much as $350. Portable units begin at about $60 and go up, depending upon size, capacity and controls.

## HOW MUCH WILL I SAVE?

Keeping the relative humidity at the optimum level should save you ten to fifteen percent of your home heating fuel bill.

---

## KEEP IT CLEAN

A humidifier must be kept clean to operate efficiently: Lime and mineral deposits can build up from the evaporation of the water in the storage tank. Add lime-combatting tablets to your humidifier, wash out the air filters and wash away excess lime deposits regularly.

# MAKING YOUR OLD FURNACE MORE EFFICIENT —BY YOURSELF

The following tips take a little more effort than turning down a thermostat, but they're well worth it:

### Remove Obstructions

All heating systems work best if the mechanism for delivering the heat is unobstructed. In a

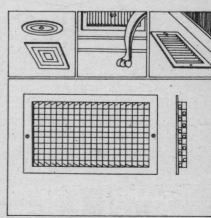

*Keep forced air ducts clean and unblocked by furniture.*

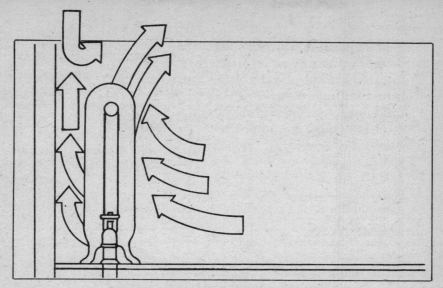

*Radiators warm through radiation and convection.*

forced-air system, this means making sure that furniture, drapes and rugs do not block the air registers. Placing a couch or bed over a register simply means you're heating upholstery, not a room. In steam and hot-water systems, you should be sure that any enclosures are removed from the radiators. It was once fashionable to build a nice, square box around radiators to hide them. Those boxes also absorb and obstruct a lot of heat that could be put to better use keeping you comfortable.

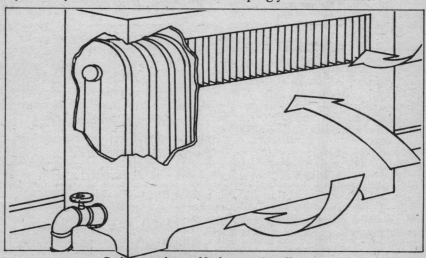

*Radiator enclosures block convection effect.*

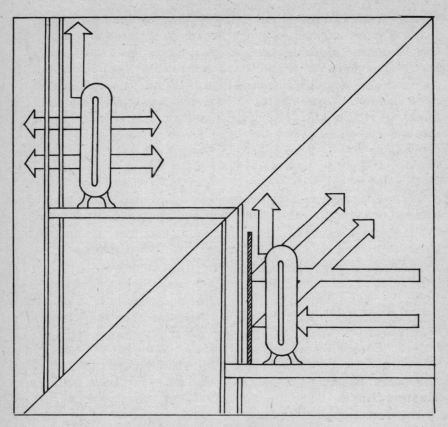

*Heat loss through exterior walls, top, can be minimized by placing a reflector behind your radiators, below.*

You can make those radiators more efficient, too, by putting a sheet of aluminum behind them to reflect heat into the room.

## Lubricate Motors

Using non-detergent motor oil from your neighborhood hardware store, lubricate your heating system's motors as indicated on the motor nameplates. This is an easy-to-forget chore, but one that will reduce friction and make your system work more efficiently. Some motors require no lubrication at all. If there are no instructions for lubricating on the motor itself, you probably have one of these.

---

**HINT**

Be careful not to overlubricate your motors. Oil can drip into areas it doesn't belong in, reducing efficiency or even causing a burn-out.

---

**70**

## Change Your Old Air Vents

If you've got a forced-air system, and some of the registers aren't adjustable, you probably find some rooms too cold and some too warm. Maybe you even things out by turning up the thermostat until the cold room is comfortable and open a window to cool down the hot room. Obviously, that's inefficient—you're heating the outside. You can balance the hot and cold rooms more inexpensively by replacing the old registers with adjustable vents and turning down the flow of hot air into the warm room. Or, you can cover part of the register in the warm room with cardboard or masking tape, forcing more of the heated air into the colder room.

## Check and Repair Heating Ducts

The ducts bringing the warm air from your furnace to your reg-

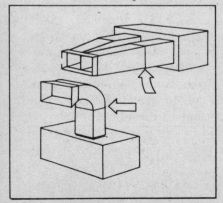

*Check hot air ducts for leaks, especially at joints.*

isters probably run through your basement or through a crawl-space. Check these ducts for air leaks, especially at the joints. If you find any, repair them with duct tape available at any hardware store.

## Change Or Clean Clogged Filters

Just like your air conditioner, your forced-air heating system has a filter to take dirt and dust

*Change forced-air heating system air filters once a month during winter.*

that's blown into your home out of the air. If that filter—located in the furnace—gets clogged, the unit will operate inefficiently and will cost you more money. One recent study indicated that a severely clogged filter (a filter with only twenty percent capacity remaining) reduced heating efficiency by 25 percent! And it's so easy to avoid this problem, it's a joke.

**71**

*Clogged filter indicator.*

Check your filter once a month and clean or change it when it gets dirty. You can tell it's dirty by holding it up to a light. If little or no light shines through, it's dirty.

If you've got the kind that can be cleaned, an inexpensive hair shampoo makes a good detergent for the filter.

**A Mechanical Aid**
You can buy and install yourself for under $20 a device that will indicate when your furnace filter is clogged and needs changing or washing. This will save you the bother of having to open up the furnace front to check your filter visually.

*Use a small piece of wood to pitch your radiators and prevent steam "banging."*

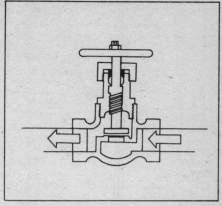

*Steam radiator valves are either "on" or "off." Turn clockwise to shut steam off. Turn counterclockwise to turn steam on. Check for leaks at the packing nut.*

## Pitch Your Radiators Properly

In a steam system, the radiators must be pitched slightly down toward the cutoff valve. This prevents the build-up of water in the radiator. Water, coming in contact with the steam, causes the annoying banging sound associated with steam heat and reduces the temperature of the steam, thus costing you more fuel. If any of your radiators are not pitched properly, you can change that by wedging small pieces of wood under the legs at the opposite end from the cutoff valve.

## Set the Cutoff Valve

The cutoff valve in a steam system is either *on* or *off*. Although there are many turns between the two, never leave the valve turned part-way. That does not allow "a little heat" into the radiator; it causes banging in the pipes and prevents the condensate from running back. *On* is counterclockwise—as far as it will go. *Off* is clockwise—as far as it will go.

### HINT

Check the cutoff valve packing on each radiator. If any of them leak steam, the tightening nut must be tightened. If it needs repacking, do it only in the summertime, when there is no steam in the system.

### KEEP IT CLEAN

A clean radiator, or hot-air register, works more efficiently than a dirty one. Vacuum radiator and register surfaces frequently.

*Periodically replace air valves on steam radiators.*

### Check and Replace Air Valves

At one end of your steam radiator you'll find an air valve—usually it looks like a miniature factory whistle. Its job is to let the cold air out of the radiator as the steam comes in. It is engineered so that it closes when the hot steam comes in contact with it—to prevent steam from escaping.

When they're working properly, these valves allow the steam to fill the radiator more quickly and under less pressure, saving energy. They must be checked and replaced periodically.

Replacement of the valves is an easy do-it-yourself project, since they screw off and on easily. Be sure to wrap the threads of the valves with dope tape to seal them.

All the air valves in a system should be replaced at once, so you maintain a balanced system. And use only quality valves—they last longer, work more efficiently and save you money in the long run.

## Bleed Radiators

An air bubble can form inside your hot-water radiators and block the flow of hot water into the unit. To "bleed" the air out, find the air valve near the top on one side of your radiator. This must usually be opened with a key or screwdriver, although some units have handles. Open the valve slowly and let the air escape. When water begins to leak out, close the valve and the radiator should work satisfactorily.

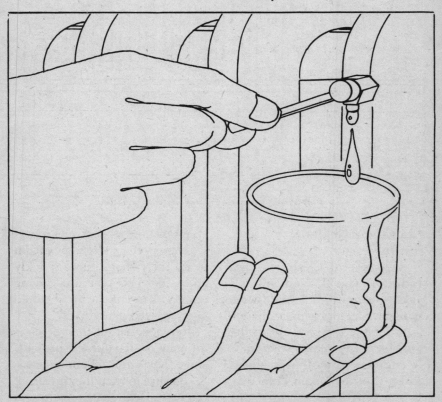

*Bleed air from hot water radiators to prevent blockage of heat.*

## Have A Tuneup

Just as your car runs more efficiently when its motor is in tune, your furnace, whether fueled by gas, oil or propane, will also operate more efficiently when it's

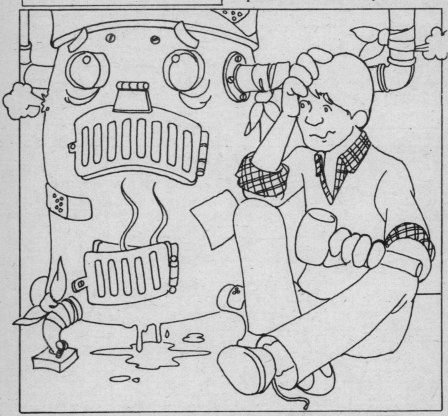

*Don't try to do-for-yourself a professional job on your heating system...But beware of who you do hire to do that work.*

## HAVING YOUR OLD FURNACE MADE MORE EFFICIENT— JOBS FOR A PROFESSIONAL

clean, lubricated and adjusted for maximum performance.

In a recent survey, 97 percent of the oil burners checked weren't firing at the correct rate and thus were wasting energy. That's a staggering number —

virtually every unit checked was wasting oil.

A simple system tuneup will pay for itself in no time. Savings from increasing the efficiency of your heating system could run as high as *thirty percent!*

## Derating

A lot of oil burners and gas furnaces are too big for the size of the area they must heat. Thus, they operate inefficiently. They quickly build up enough heat for a house, then they shut down.

To put it in automobile terms, it's like having a Cadillac motor in a Volkswagen. You won't get where you're going any faster, if you observe the speed limit, but you'll waste an awful lot of gas doing it.

Many furnaces with excess capacity operate only thirty percent of the time, even in the coldest winter months. During the off-cycle, heat is lost up the flue and through the furnace walls into the adjacent area.

One way of combatting excess capacity is by "derating" your unit, putting a smaller nozzle on the burner, which means it will operate longer, but use less fuel.

## Get An Automatic Flue Damper

When your furnace is in its off-cycle—and even the most efficient units have off-cycles—

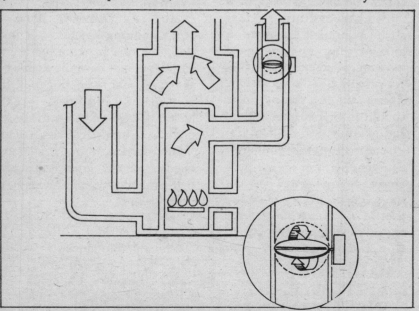

*How an automatic flue damper works. In off cycle damper closes flue, keeps heat in the furnace. In on cycle, it opens to allow combustion gases to escape.*

## WHAT WILL IT COST?

An automatic flue damper will cost you between $250 and $500 installed, depending on the model you chose and the difficulty of installation on your furnace.

## HOW MUCH WILL I SAVE?

Depending on your unit, you'll save ten to fifteen percent (units with longer off-cycles save more).

## CAUTION

An automatic flue damper should be installed *only* by a skilled, reputable, professional contractor. Dampers on gas-burning units should have an endorsement from the American Gas Association. Those on oil-burning units should have an Underwriters Laboratory label. Do not attempt to install your own flue damper and do not purchase any damper that does not have the necessary endorsement. An improperly-designed or improperly-installed flue damper can be very dangerous.

heat is lost up the flue pipe. This can be remedied with a newly popular device called a flue damper. Simply put, the damper closes the flue when the furnace is off and reopens it when the furnace kicks on. Thus, when no heat is being generated, the system remains closed. And when the fire restarts, the flue opens to exhaust the poisonous gases produced by the furnace.

## Have Hanging Baffles Installed

Just as a hat keeps in your body heat on a cold winter's day, a hanging baffle keeps a "lid" on your furnace's fire—containing and concentrating it so it isn't dissipated up the flue.

A hanging baffle is a stone box suspended by chains over the combustion chamber.

Modern furnaces do not require hanging baffles, but installation of a hanging baffle in an old unit may save you as much as ten percent in heating fuel. If you have an old furnace that looks like one of those in these pictures—they're called vertical boilers—have your serviceman check it for a hanging baffle and, if it doesn't have one, consider ordering one.

## Install A Return Air Duct

On older forced-air and hot-air systems, the room air is returned to the furnace through a large vent in the floor. This air

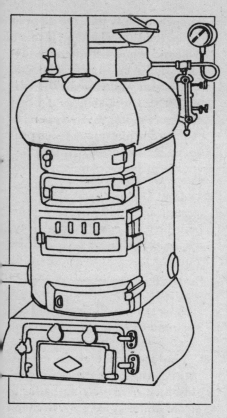
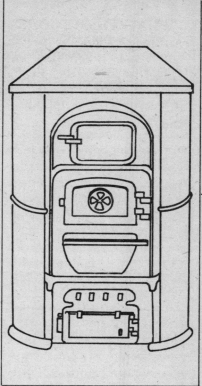

*Vertical boilers. Check for hanging baffles.*

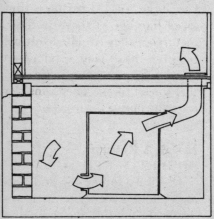
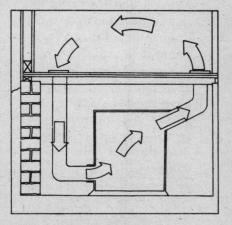

*Hot air system without return air duct. Hot air system with return air duct.*

mingles with the cold basement air before it gets to the furnace to be reheated. On newer systems the room air is returned to the furnace through a duct. Thus, the furnace doesn't have to work as hard since it's not warming a lot of basement air.

If your system doesn't have a return air duct, consider having one installed. The savings should be substantial, although they are impossible to estimate, since they vary according to the conditions in each basement. In some extreme cases, however, you can cut your fuel bill nearly in half!

## A FRINGE BENEFIT

If you're no longer heating basement air, your house will be *cleaner*, as well as warmer. Without all that basement dirt and dust circulating through your forced-air system, you'll save your own, personal energy by not having to work as hard cleaning. (And you'll save electricity, too, since you won't have to run your vacuum cleaner as much.)

That takes care of your primary heating system. It's time to see how we get some heat, as well as some light, from—

## BE A SKEPTIC

No matter how altruistic they may sound, bear in mind that your utility and your oil delivery firm are in business to *sell* you fuel, not to *save* you fuel.

When selecting someone to inspect, repair or upgrade your heating system, you may be much better off engaging an independent who comes to you without a built-in conflict-of-interest. If his business is solely furnace maintenance and repair—and not fuel sales—he's earning his money by saving yours.

## —YOUR FIREPLACE

Remember those knights and their ladies in that European castle practically standing in their giant, walk-in fireplaces to keep warm? Well, the warmest part of the castle was really the flue—because that's where most of the heat went.

And it's little different today. Unless you live in the flue, you don't get a lot of heat from your fireplace. (And, of course, you couldn't live in the flue, even if you could fit, because in addition to heat, there's a lot of deadly gas coming up that chimney.)

That cheery fire may warm your heart on a cold winter

night, but unless you take certain steps, that's all it'll warm. In fact, a fireplace—even with a fire going—can sometimes cost you heating dollars, because your gas- or oil-fired heat is escaping up that flue right along with the wood-fired heat. And after the wood fire goes out, that open flue is as bad as a hole in the roof.

An open flue can cost you more than $100 a year in fuel bills.

## Close That Damper

A lot of fireplace flues have built-in dampers—a kind of door in the flue that closes it off to the outside. If your fireplace has such a door, *close it* when the fireplace isn't in use. But don't try to close the damper all the way when there is a fire going—you'll fill your house with smoke and combustion gases.

If your fireplace was built with no damper, you can have one installed. The cost will vary

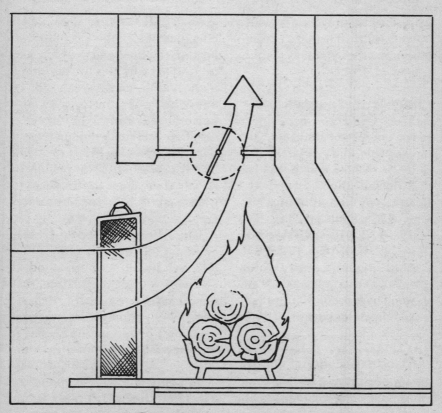

*Heated room air escapes up your open fireplace flue damper.*

between about $150 and $300, depending on the individual problems your contractor will encounter with your particular fireplace.

Even if you have a damper, however, there are drawbacks. If you go to bed at night with the fire still smoldering, you have to leave th  damper open—and that means room heat will escape up the flue when the fire finally does go out. Also, it's pretty easy to forget to close most dampers—since they're up the flue, they're generally out of sight. There are some other remedies you may want to consider.

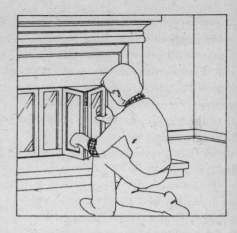

*Glass fireplace doors prevent heat loss.*

### Close off the Fireplace

Shove fiberglass up the flue to block the loss of warm air. You obviously can't do this if the fireplace is to be used, but if you can do without a fire in the hearth, you can save heat this way. REMEMBER TO REMOVE THE FIBERGLASS BEFORE BUILDING A FIRE!

Fiberglass is really a temporary solution. There are permanent solutions that are most costly, but are easier to live with.

### Glass Fireplace Doors

Despite the claims of manufacturers, glass fireplace doors or screens don't increase the radiant heat your fireplace will give off. However, they will effectively block the exit of room heat up the flue, will enable you to go off to bed with a fire burning in the hearth, increase safety because they lessen the risk of burning logs rolling out of the fireplace and don't diminish the beauty of a roaring fire.

A fringe benefit is they cut the supply of oxygen to the fire somewhat, making the wood burn longer.

Glass fireplace screens cost around $200 and can be installed by most handy do-it-yourselfers. For others, installation charges are usually nominal, since it usually takes only an hour for a professional to install the screen.

### Wood-Stove Fireplace Insert

From the outside, a wood-stove fireplace insert doesn't look much different from a fireplace outfitted with glass doors. But there is a major difference: A stove-like device has been inserted into the hearth and, through convection, as well as through radiation, it makes the wood fire far more efficient and heat-producing.

These units, although costly, can eventually pay for themselves. Some offer fan attachments to enhance the convection function (sometimes called "induced convection").

## WOOD-BURNING STOVES

The wood-burning stove probably originated in the seventeenth century, but went into a decline in this country with the advent of coal, and later oil and gas, heat.

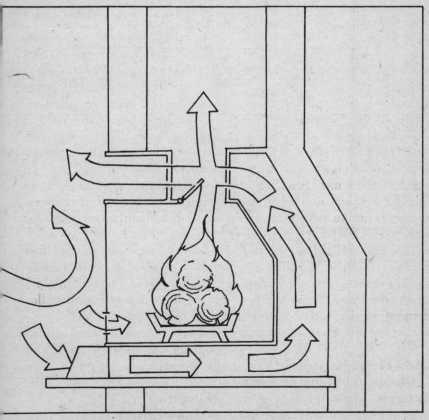

*Woodburning stove fireplace insert heats by convection.*

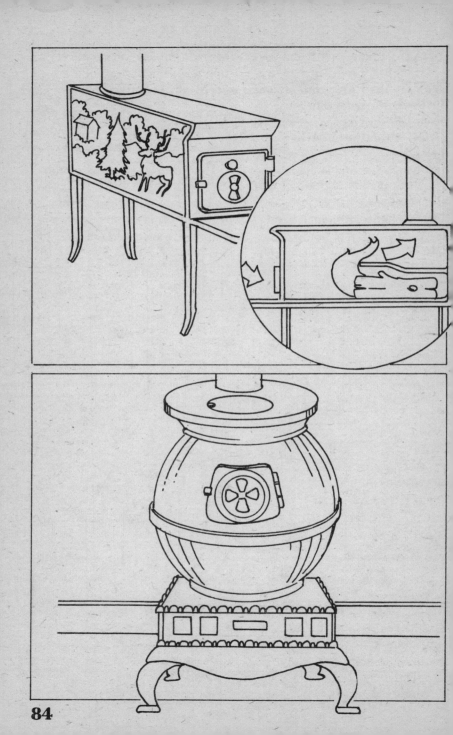

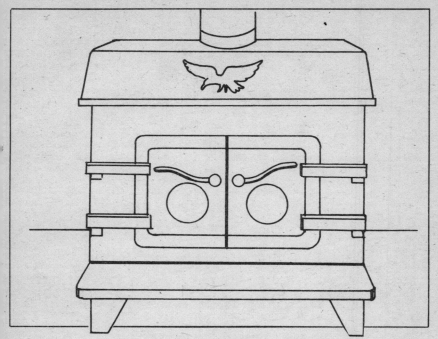

*Three common types of radiant-heat wood stoves.*

However, wood is making a comeback, especially in modern, efficient wood-burning stoves. Typically, these units are used to supplement gas, oil or electric heat in homes. They are far more economical in rural than in urban areas, because firewood prices are so much lower (if it isn't free!), but even in bustling suburbs, more and more homeowners are installing wood-burning stoves.

All wood-burning stoves supply radiant heat. The cast-iron or steel sides of the stove get hot and the heat radiates off the surface and into the room. As with any other radiant-heat method, the air is warmest closer to the source of the heat. In fact, stoves can become dangerously hot and should never be touched while a fire is burning in them.

Some of the newer stoves work by convection as well. These units have cavities around the firebox that create a convection flow of air. Cold air goes into the cavities at the bottom of the stove, is exposed to the heat of the fire (but not to the smoke or gases) and is expelled into the room at the top or sides. Some convection models have fans to induce more room air through the cavities.

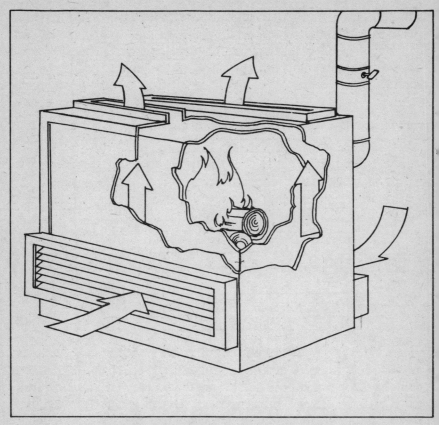

*How a modern convection and radiant heat wood stove works.*

## Wood-Stove Safety

Wood stoves can be dangerous. If you follow these basic safety tips, you should get a lot of secure enjoyment and supplementary heat from your wood stove.

———

— Don't use cardboard boxes or wooden boxes to store ashes. Use only metal containers.

— Don't use more than one heating unit for each chimney flue.

— Don't use masonry chimneys that do not have a flue tile lining.

— Don't use units where the flue pipe is loose and is not connected properly.

— Don't use chimney flues unless they are at least two or three feet above roof.

— Don't use chimneys if they do not have a fly-ash or spark screen.

— Don't use stove on combustible floors: wood, asphalt, tile, etc.

— Don't use metal chimneys if not insulated away from wood-framed structures.

— Don't place furnishings or carpeting near through-floor chimneys.

— Don't place combustibles such as liquid, flammables, paper, cloth, etc. too close to stove or chimneys.

— Don't dry wood, paper, clothing or any combustibles on stove.

## NUTS TO YOUR FIRE!

Does your fire dwindle down to virtually nothing after a few minutes? Is it lazy, lethargic and not very bright? Well, nuts to it! Or, more accurately, nut-shells. Nutshells are hard and dense and burn brightly and hotly. Save nutshells and use them for both starting your fireplace fire and for reviving it when it begins to die out.

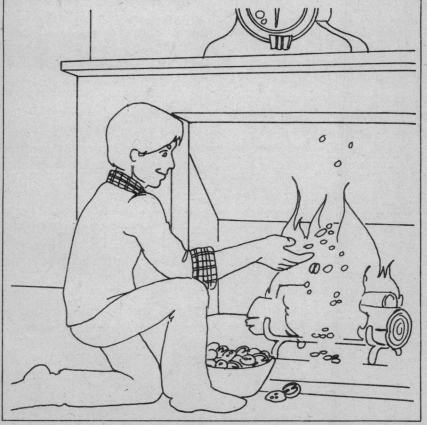

— Don't use chimneys or stoves that are coated with creosote.

—Don't install any stove or chimney without consulting your local or municipal codes.

—Don't use liquid flammables to fuel or light stove.

—Don't use charcoal as a fuel.

—Don't use hard or soft coal.

—Don't use units unless checked for cracks.

—Don't use units unless they are placed more than three feet from any combustible wall.

— Don't touch surface of stove while in use.

— Don't service hot units while wearing loose clothing.

— Don't permit children to play near unattended units.

— Don't use green wood.

— Don't use units as an incinerator.

— Don't use units without fire extinguishers or a bucket of sand or water nearby.

— Don't buy units that are oversize for the area to be heated.

— Don't use or install smoke pipes that extend more than ten feet horizontally.

— Don't place stove pipes closer than 18 inches to any combustible material.

—Don't use plastic piping or any other combustible material for stove pipes.

— Don't use any stove unless it's been approved by a testing laboratory.

# HOW ECONOMICAL IS IT?

The cost of wood as a fuel varies so greatly around the country, it is impossible to generalize about how economical it is.

If you live in the heart of a big city, where nothing grows but lightpoles, fire hydrants and parking meters — and the nearest forest is some distance away — wood isn't going to be economical.

If you live in the backwoods, with a forest at your door, all the fuel will cost you will be the sweat of your brow (or maybe a little gasoline, if you use a chain saw).

Wherever you live and however you get your wood, remember that dry wood is best and split wood burns better than unsplit, round logs.

Dry — or seasoned — wood has generally been cut and stacked and left standing in a dry place for ten months to a year. The dry wood will leave less soot in your chimney and will burn hotter.

Softer woods — pines, firs, other evergreens — start fast but burn very quickly. Hard woods —oak, ash, maple—are harder to start, but since the wood is denser, their fires last longer.

Generally speaking, a cord of

## Characteristics of Commonly Burned Fuel Woods

### HARDWOODS

| Species | Length of Burning | Ease of Starting |
|---|---|---|
| Oak | Excellent | Poor |
| Birch (white) | Good | Good |
| Ash | Good | Fair |
| Maple (sugar) | Good | Poor |
| Elm | Fair | Fair |

### SOFTWOODS

| Species | Length of Burning | Ease of Starting |
|---|---|---|
| Fir | Fair | Good |
| Hemlock | Fair | Good |
| Spruce | Fair | Good |
| Cedar | Poor | Excellent |
| Pine (white) | Poor | Excellent |

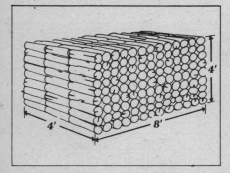

*A cord of wood measures four feet by eight feet by four feet.*

wood has about the same heat-producing power as 200 gallons of heating oil, when the wood is burned in an efficient stove. But what is a cord of wood? A cord of wood is 128 cubic feet of wood.

Put in more understandable terms, it is a stack of logs four feet deep, four feet high and eight feet long.

A good supply of dry firewood, an efficient wood-burning stove and a few other precautions can save your life — and your family's lives—in a fuel emergency.

While it may seem unlikely that all sources of heating fuel will be totally cut off, it once seemed unlikely that we'd be paying more than a dollar for a gallon of gasoline. The unexpected has a nasty habit of happening. This next section could save your life—

# —THE WORST POSSIBLE CONDITIONS—

## SURVIVING WITHOUT FUEL IN AN EMERGENCY

It's winter. A blizzard has struck, and you're stuck in your home. The power lines have gone down and there is no electricity. Foreign suppliers have cut America's access to imported oil. Saboteurs have severed the major gas pipelines. It is 15 degrees outside.

Are you prepared for an all-encompassing emergency like that? Will you starve first or freeze first? Or will you make it through with minimal inconvenience?

Here's how to survive the worst possible conditions:

### PLAN AHEAD

Every home should have the following equipment:

• An emergency food and water supply. The food should be canned, jarred or boxed goods that need no refrigeration. Buy high-energy foods (raisins, other dried fruit, honey, etc.) to help you keep warm; paper plates and

*Stock up on high-energy foods.*

cups (every meal will become a picnic).

• A first-aid kit consisting of compress bandages of various sizes, plain gauze, a tourniquet, scissors, tweezers and wood splints and a Red Cross or Boy Scout first-aid manual.

• Alternate lighting equipment — flashlights, extra batteries (keep batteries in plastic bags in your freezer to extend their shelf life), candles, matches, hurricane lanterns with kerosene. (Boy Scout flashlights are par-

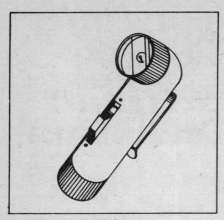

*A Boy Scout flashlight.*

ticularly good since they can be used as lamps or hooked to a belt to free your hands while they light your way.)

EMERGENCY LIST
POLICE        999 1602
FIRE DEPT.   761-6801
AMBULANCE - 761-7770
HOSPITAL    999 3023
NEIGHBORS 608 4011'
MOM         761 2000
GAS CO.      999 111 6
ELECTRIC CO. 761-00
WATER CO.   608-0

• Emergency phone numbers (in case phone service is restored).

• Battery-powered radio with plenty of extra batteries. (With the phone lines out, the radio will be your only contact with the outside world.)

• Extra blankets and/or sleeping bags (down-filled are warmest).

• An alternate heating source (a wood-burning stove with an ample supply of seasoned wood; a clean, well-functioning fireplace; kerosene, gasoline or propane space heaters with lots of fuel).

• Fire-fighting equipment — Fire extinguishers, buckets of sand, a shovel, an ax. The alternate heating sources should present no danger if properly used —but you *must* be ready to deal with accidental fires.

• Extra supplies of any prescription medicine for family members taking medication.

• Warm clothing—Wool is best, layers are more effective than bulky single garments. Wool hats are critical (we lose half our body heat through uncovered heads). Longjohns are worth their weight in oil.

• Ample supplies of newspaper, clear plastic wrap, tape (for wrapping your water pipes to prevent freezing).

• Automobile anti-freeze for toilet tanks, dishwashers, hard-to-reach drains.

• Cards, games, books—to keep you and your family from contracting cabin fever.

Taking these steps in advance will improve your ability to weather the ultimate storm—

## —WHEN IT HAPPENS

Okay, you're prepared. Now it happens. There's snow up to

your shoulders outside and no power, no telephone, no heat. What do you do?

- Pull the plugs. Unplug electrical appliances. Turn off your furnace's electrical starter. You don't want them damaged by a power surge when the electricity comes back on line.

- Keep your freezer closed. Use only food from the refrigerator. This will keep spoilage to a minimum. (After the emergency, refreeze only those items that still have ice crystals on them. Otherwise, keep foods refrigerated or prepare them. If the crisis lasts too long, throw out possibly spoiled food. There is no sense risking illness by eating foods that may have gone bad.)

- *Don't* drink alcoholic beverages or take tranquilizing drugs. They slow down body functions and you'll be colder.

- Wrap any uninsulated water pipes in newspaper and cover the newspaper with plastic, to combat the possibility of their freezing. Open taps a little to keep water running. It will waste water, but so will a burst pipe. If it gets below freezing in the house, you may have to shut off your water from its source and drain all pipes. If you're doing that, be sure you empty out drain traps and the hoses behind your washing

*Insulate water pipes with newspaper and plastic wrap.*

machine. Put automotive antifreeze in your toilet bowls and tanks to keep them from freezing. You can pour a little into your dishwasher, if you have one, and into hard-to-reach drains. (Be sure to run the dishwasher without dishes after the emergency to purge the anti-freeze.)

- Hang blankets over your windows at night to keep cold air out, heat in. Take them down during the day to get the sun's radiant heat.

- Shut off rooms and centralize family life around the alternate heating source.

- Dress warmly and wear a wool hat—even when you sleep.

*Stay close together to conserve body heat.*

*Emergency lamps.*

- Several light blankets are more effective than a single thick blanket. Bunch together to preserve body heat.
- Try to stay dry, try to stay indoors.

*Stay indoors, stay warm, stay dry.*

## EMERGENCY LIGHTING

You can make your candles last longer by putting them in a glass and filling the glass two-thirds full of cooking oil. When the candle burns down to the oil, it will turn into an oil lamp and

should last for days as the oil burns instead of the wick.

You can make an emergency "Aladdin's lamp" from a creamer, a piece of cotton rag and some peanut or other cooking oil.

Fill the creamer with oil, cut the rag into a wick with a piece hanging over the edge of the spout and place the creamer on a larger dish, to prevent dripping. Light the wick and refill the oil as it burns down.

## EXPOSURE TREATMENT

Prolonged exposure to cold and wet weather can be serious and even life-threatening. Often, the person suffering exposure doesn't realize he or she is in trouble.

If you are exposed to too much cold and wet, get into dry clothing as quickly as possible. Apply a warm hot water bottle or warm, dry towels to the trunk of your body. Raise your feet slight-

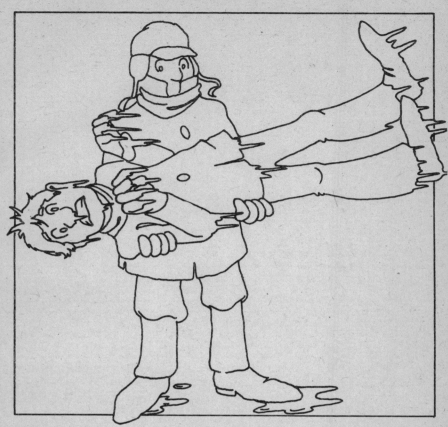

ly to keep blood circulating to the brain. Drink warm drinks (but not alcoholic drinks). Remain quiet. Avoid massages or rubbing—they can do more harm than good.

Probably, you will never face an emergency this dire, but you've got real problems to face every day, such as—

# —FEEDING ENERGY-HUNGRY MOUTHS:

## Your Appliances

In any family there can be children who are picky eaters, hardly touching their food, and other children who seem to have bottomless pits for stomachs.

It's the same way with those dozens of electric appliances you've got around your house. Some of them have really voracious appetites, some use very little power.

One way to save is to use the energy-gorgers as little as possible. The following list includes the most common appliances along with their *annual* estimated electricity consumption in kilowatt hours.

To work out the actual cost to you, call your local utility and ask what you are charged per kilowatt hour (the figure is never printed on your utility bill — making electricity one of the few commodities we buy without ever seeing the price tag!). Now multiply the rate by the kilowatt hour consumption of the appliance and you'll have a ballpark estimate of what your actual dollar costs are for each appliance. (Of course, the cost will vary according to the size of the appliance and the amount of usage. If you leave your television on all day, you'll use more than the "average usage" figure cited in the chart.)

|  | Est. kWh used annually |
|---|---|
| **Major Appliances** | |
| Air-Conditioner (room) | 860 |
| (Based on 1000 hours of operation per year. This figure will vary widely depending on geographic area and specific size of unit) | |

| | Est. kWh used annually |
|---|---:|
| Clothes Dryer | 993 |
| Dishwasher | |
| Including energy used to heat water | 2,100 |
| Dishwasher only | 363 |
| Freezer (16 cu. ft.) | 1,190 |
| Freezer—frostless (16.5 cu. ft.) | 1,820 |
| Range with oven | 700 |
| with self-cleaning oven | 730 |
| Refrigerator (12 cu. ft.) | 728 |
| Refrigerator—frostless (12 cu. ft.) | 1,217 |
| Refrigerator/Freezer (12.5 cu. ft.) | 1,500 |
| Refrigerator/Freezer—frostless (17.5 cu. ft.) | 2,250 |
| Washing machine | |
| Including energy used to heat water | 2,500 |
| Washing machine only | 103 |
| Water Heater | 4,811 |

**Kitchen Appliances**

| | |
|---|---:|
| Blender | 15 |
| Broiler | 100 |
| Carving Knife | 8 |
| Coffee Maker | 140 |
| Deep Fryer | 83 |

| | Est. kWh used annually |
|---|---|
| Egg Cooker | 14 |
| Frying Pan | 186 |
| Hot Plate | 90 |
| Mixer | 13 |
| Microwave Oven | 190 |
| Roaster | 205 |
| Sandwich Grill | 33 |
| Toaster | 39 |
| Trash Compactor | 50 |
| Waffle Iron | 22 |
| Waste Disposer | 30 |

## Heating and Cooling

| | |
|---|---|
| Air Cleaner | 216 |
| Electric Blanket | 147 |
| Dehumidifier | 377 |
| Fan (attic) | 291 |
| Fan (circulating) | 43 |
| Fan (rollaway) | 138 |
| Fan (window) | 170 |
| Heater (portable) | 176 |
| Heating Pad | 10 |
| Humidifier | 163 |

## Laundry

| | |
|---|---|
| Iron | 144 |

## Health & Beauty

| | |
|---|---|
| Electric Toothbrush | .5 |
| Germicidal Lamp | 141 |
| Hair Dryer | 14 |
| Heat Lamp (infrared) | 13 |
| Shaver | 1.8 |
| Sun Lamp | 16 |

## Home Entertainment

| | |
|---|---|
| Radio | 86 |
| Radio/Record Player | 109 |
| Television | |
| Black & white | |
| Tube type | 350 |
| Solid state | 120 |
| Color | |
| Tube type | 660 |
| Solid state | 440 |

## Housewares

| | |
|---|---|
| Clock | 17 |
| Floor Polisher | 15 |
| Sewing Machine | 11 |
| Vacuum Cleaner | 46 |

*Source: Edison Electric Institute

## THE CODE OF THE WEST—AND EAST, NORTH AND SOUTH

EER—Energy Efficiency Rating—is the new code of the West—and the East, the North and the South.

Under the law, manufacturers of major appliances must list an energy efficiency rating on their products, so you can compare them with similar products of other manufacturers and buy those that will be most economical to operate.

The EER is assigned to products by the Federal Government after testing.

The following appliances *must* display an EER label:

Central and room air conditioners

Clothes washers and dryers

Dishwashers

Freezers and refrigerators

Furnaces and other home heating equipment

Humidifiers and dehumidifiers

Kitchen ranges and ovens

Water heaters

Television sets

Be an energy-conscious consumer; use the EER label for comparison purposes when you buy.

Of course, if you're not in the market for a new refrigerator, air conditioner or range right now, you'll want to know about—

## —GETTING MORE EFFICIENCY FROM YOUR OLD APPLIANCES

We use energy to run a variety of appliances—everything from the essential—such as water heaters—to the frivolous—such as the video games.

The more we conserve on any of these appliances, the more we save in dollar terms and in terms of our country's dependence on foreign suppliers of energy fuels.

The largest energy-eater among our household appliances is—

## THE WATER HEATER

It probably doesn't cross your mind when you open that hot water tap to do the dishes or to fill your bathtub, but *fifteen percent* of all the energy used in your home goes for making that water hot.

So any savings we can register in this area will be substantial, whether we heat our water with gas, electricity or oil.

Here's how to save some money on your hot water fuel bill:

**Lower the water temperature.** You burn more fuel or use more electricity to get that water to a higher temperature. A setting of 160°F, while common, is too hot. You don't need water that hot and you can scald yourself

**101**

with it. So for safety's sake, as well as for conservation's sake, you should lower that water temperature. How far? Well, dropping the temperature from 160 to 140 will save you about eighteen percent of your water-heating bill. Dropping it another twenty degrees, to 120, can save you another eighteen percent. And 120 ought to be adequate for most household needs, except for dishwashers, which generally need water of 140° to operate properly.

All water heaters have a temperature control somewhere on them. Some are marked off in degrees and are quite easy to lower to the exact temperature you want. Others, however, have controls marked "high" and "low," with a variety of settings in between. If yours is one of these, drop the control back a couple notches and then test the water temperature with a meat thermometer. If it is still too high, lower it another notch, and so on until you get the temperature you want.

This is a no-investment measure—it costs you nothing but a few minutes of your time and begins saving you money at once.

**Insulate Your Hot Water Heater.** Hot water heaters contain insulation, but if you can feel heat through the unit's walls, then it can benefit from additional, exterior insulation. (In almost all cases insulation will help. And, like chicken soup, it can't hurt—if applied correctly.)

This is one of the easiest money-saving ideas; a quick, inexpensive, do-it-yourself project that will cost you about $15 for an insulation kit and half an hour of your time. It can save you its purchase price in the first year of operation.

The kit, available in hardware and building supply stores, is really a fiberglass overcoat for the water heater. It can be used on any kind of water heater, but the manufacturer's instructions *must* be followed to the letter to eliminate the risk of fire. The vent or flue at the top of gas- and oil-fired heaters should not be blocked, and the control and terminal boxes on electrical heaters cannot be covered or the wiring will overheat.

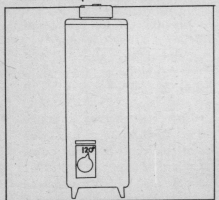

*Lower your water heater temperature.*

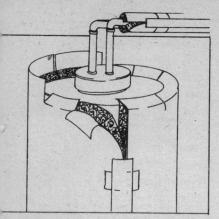

*Insulate hot water heater and your hot water pipes.*

*Drain sediment from your hot water heater.*

## Insulate Your Hot Water Pipes.

As the hot water flows through unheated areas to sinks and bathtubs, some heat is lost by radiant action through the pipes. This can be prevented by insulating your hot water pipes (you should also insulate cold water pipes to eliminate condensation). Insulation designed specifically for water pipes is available at hardware and building supply stores. In most cases you'll have to wrap fiberglass or a similar material around the pipes and then cover it with plastic or some other airtight material. There are also kits of pre-formed foam insulation that snaps around the pipes. This type is far quicker to install, although it is more expensive.

## Drain Sediment from Your Water Heater.

Sediment at the bottom of the tank in your hot water heater acts as an insulation barrier *between* your heat source and the water—cutting your unit's efficiency. Every couple of months, drain off a gallon or two of water from the valve at the bottom of the tank to eliminate this sediment.

---

### CAUTION

Remember the insulation-handling precautions: Wear long sleeves, a dust mask and gloves.

---

## Clean Heating Elements Once a Year.

That same sediment can corrode the heating elements in your electric hot water heater, making them less efficient. Once a year, cut the power to the unit, close the inlet valve, drain the tank and carefully remove the heating elements (there should be two—one at the middle of the tank, the other at the bottom). Clean off the corrosion with a wire brush and replace the elements. Be sure you let the tank fill with water before you turn the electricity back on, to keep the elements from over-heating.

**Install an Automatic Flue Damper.** In gas-and-oil-fired hot water heaters, a lot of the flame's heat can be lost up the flue, just as it can be in a furnace. The remedy is the same—have an automatic flue damper installed. They are less expensive than those for a furnace—running about $150 to $200—and they should save you ten to fifteen percent of your water heating costs.

**Fix Those Leaks.** In addition to making maddening drip-drip-drip noise all night, a leaky hot-water faucet can cost you

*A drip that fills a cup every ten minutes wastes more than 3,000 gallons of hot water a year.*

money. If you've got a drop-per-second leak you're losing 3,120

gallons of hot water a year *and* the money it took to heat those gallons. Replacing a washer (the most common cause of a faucet drip) costs practically nothing and takes very little time.

**Add Aerators and Flow Restrictors.** Aerators introduce air into the flow of water at the faucet. While you perceive an undiminished flow of water and substantial pressure, actually less water is being used—thus you save on heating the water you *don't* use. Install aerators and flow restrictors in all sinks and shower heads.

**Take Showers.** As long as we're in the shower, let's take one. Showers use less water than baths (as long as you don't take inordinately long showers). Encourage your family to take showers to save on hot water. (And if you really want to save, try taking a "Navy shower." Aboard ship, where fresh water is at a premium, sailors wet themselves down and turn off the shower while they soap up. Then they turn the shower back on to rinse. In a Navy or even a civilian shower, the faster you move, the more you save.)

**Fill Those Washers.** It takes as much hot water to run a dishwasher or clothes washer through a cycle when it is half-loaded as it does when it is fully loaded, so wait until you've got those appliances filled up before running them. You'll do fewer washes, save on hot water and save on electricity, too. (Also, your machines will last longer because they'll run less.)

**Cold-Water Washes.** Wash clothes in cold water whenever possible. Or use a warm wash, but *avoid* a hot-water wash. Use the proper detergent and you'll still get clean garments. A lot of newer garments can be rinsed in cold water, so save by shutting off the hot water in the rinse cycle when you can.

And when you're buying clothing, read the care label—and seek out cold-water washables. (No-iron garments save you the electricity you'd use on ironing—not to mention the dismal drudgery of the chore.)

**Buy the Right Water Heater.** When your old water heater wears out, buy the right-size replacement for your home. Too much capacity means too much wasted energy. If you've got a three-bedroom, two-bathroom home, you're wasting money if you buy an 80-gallon unit, both when you purchase it and when you operate it.

If you aren't getting enough hot water from your present unit, you may not have to replace it. Frequently, you can save by

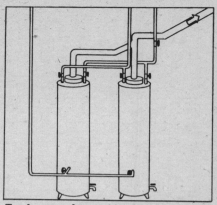

*Two hot water heaters in series may save you money.*

buying a same-size unit and hooking it up parallel to your existing unit.(For example, two thirty-gallon heaters may be more efficient—and less expensive—than a single new sixty-gallon unit.)

## WHAT ABOUT THE SUN?

The sun's radiant energy is free. The equipment necessary to convert it to water heating isn't. The present state of the art is such that a solar hot-water system can provide half or more of your family's hot water, reducing your total fuel bill by about ten percent. They cost upwards of $2,500, installed.

Now we've heated things up, it's time to talk about playing it—

## —COOL, MAN, COOL: AIR CONDITIONING AND VENTILATION

In the days of cheap energy, we grew to think of air conditioning as a necessity. But there are some of us who remember the days when it wasn't even a luxury—when it didn't exist at all. Somehow, mankind survived! So, in this day and age, we can certainly take a little more heat before we get out of the kitchen (or turn on our air conditioners); we can operate them at lower levels; we can ventilate our homes naturally and we can save a lot of money, too. Even the most efficient air conditioners are relatively expensive appliances to operate since they are heat-transfer machines with heavy-duty motors. So the less we use them, the more we save. And the more efficient we make our air conditioners, the more we save.

### Tolerating Higher Temperatures

The government recommends keeping air-conditioned buildings at temperatures no cooler than 78°F. That's warm, but livable. For every degree you raise the temperature in an air-conditioned room, you'll save two to three percent of your cooling costs. So if you go from the old standard of 72 to the new recommendation of 78, you'll save a whopping twelve to eighteen percent!

## SERVICING YOUR AIR CONDITIONER

If you've got an air conditioner, you're going to use it. So let's use it in the most economical way possible. Keep it running smoothly, cleanly and efficiently, and it'll do the job of cooling you a lot cheaper than if you don't maintain it. And *you* can do a lot of the maintenance, whether you've got central air conditioning or individual window units.

All air conditioners should be serviced at least once a year. Motors should be lubricated, coils cleaned and filters checked and changed.

Coils? Motors? Filters? What and where?

Well, all air conditioners operate as heat extractors and humidity extractors. They suck warm, moist air out of the room or house, remove the heat and moisture and dissipate them outside the structure. Dirt will hinder the flow of the hot air—making the unit work longer — and will prevent condensation of the moisture.

**Filters:** Filters in window units should be cleaned or replaced

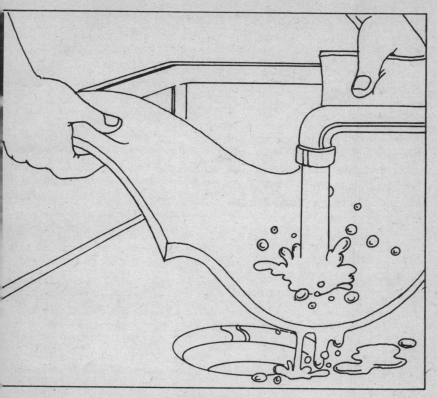

*Wash air conditioner filters once a month.*

once a month during the cooling season. Foam filters can be cleaned by washing them in liquid detergent or — even better — an inexpensive shampoo. You can replace the washed filter while it's still damp.

Replace the filters on central air conditioners once a month. Most units have two filters and replacements should cost you about $1 for each filter. Again, be certain the unit is shut off before you open it up to extract the filter. Anyone can do this job — it's simple. But it's also easy to forget. Remember those filters!

## Economy Runs

On really hot days, run the air conditioner with the fan set on high. In very humid weather, set the fan at low speed to provide more moisture removal, but less cooling. You can feel comfortable at higher temperatures if the air's less humid.

## Shut It Off

It is *not* more economical to leave an air conditioner on all day. A machine doesn't have to work longer to cool a hot room than to maintain a constant cool temperature in a room. So if you're leaving the house — or temporarily quitting an air-conditioned room — save yourself some dollars by turning off the air conditioner.

## Be A Cool Customer

When shopping for an air conditioner, check the EER of the unit. The higher the EER, the more efficient (and money saving) the unit. Also, buy air conditioners that are adequate for the job, but not overpowered machines. The smallest capacity unit for the job is the best one. More cooling power than you need is inefficient.

**108**

## STORM WINDOWS IN SUMMER?

When running your air conditioners, be sure to keep doors and windows closed. And, ironically, those storm windows you installed to keep out the stiff winter winds can keep the cool air-conditioned breezes inside during the summer.

**Coils:** The air conditioner coils are heat exchangers. Interior coils absorb heat, exterior coils expel it. Dirt build-up on the coils acts as insulation, hindering both functions. Clean internal coils with a damp rag or a soft brush then vacuum. And you can hose down the external coils while you're watering your lawn or washing your car.

## Shade It

The ideal location for an air conditioner is the north side of a building or in the shade. If that is impossible, consider installing an awning over an air conditioner. The less heat hitting the unit outside the house, the easier it is for the machine to dissipate heat from inside the house.

*Keep your air conditioners clean.*

*Shading an air conditioner will increase its efficiency.*

**109**

# BE A FAN OF A FAN

Remember fans? Sure you do. They used to work. They still do. Even better today, because they've been scientifically improved. And an attic fan can ventilate your whole house and reduce the burden of your air conditioner by as much as 25 percent. (And that means on those marginal air-conditioning days, you won't need the air conditioner at all; you'll be able to cool by ventilating.) A big attic fan has a motor rated at about 1/4 to 1/3 horsepower. By contrast, an air-conditioner motor can be anywhere from one full horsepower, to three or four horses. It's obvious that it's less expensive to feed 1/3 of a horse than three horses, so a fan can save you a lot of money (an air conditioner can use as much as *ten times* the expensive electricity that a big attic fan uses).

**Where Should You Put Your Fan?** For a really good do-it-yourselfer, installing an attic fan is a challenging project. For most homeowners, though, it's a job for professionals.

Where do you put that fan? Well, the most effective spot is on an exterior wall either at the gable end or between the rafters of your roof. Units installed in the attic floor aren't as effective,

but still do help ventilate a house.

---

### CAUTION

I recommend installing an attic fan with a thermostat—one that switches itself on when the temperature in the attic climbs above 100°F. But it must also have a safety disconnect device so that it shuts off in the event of a fire in the house. A running ventilator fan will make a fire more intense by drawing oxygen into the building.

---

**Fan It Again, Sam.** Those lazy-moving ceiling fans you remember in *Casablanca* were there mostly for atmosphere. But if you install one or two they'll stir up a pleasant breeze to combat the summer's heat. They really work. (Would Bogie install a dud in Rick's Café Américain?)

## ADDITIONAL VENTILATION

You'll have to take pains to see that all closed spaces and dead air spaces in your home—such as attic areas, crawlspaces, cocklofts, and underground vaults—have some ventilation all year round to permit a free flow of fresh air and to allow moisture to dissipate. The ventilator can be as simple as a small grille covered with screening to prevent insects and vermin from getting in your home.

### Nature's Own

Hot air rises, right? Well, not exactly. Hot air is forced up by cooler air—which is heavier.

Why am I telling you all this? Why do you need to know it? So you'll be able to follow the

*Natural ventilation flow.*

reasoning behind a natural ventilation system that uses no fans at all.

On the north side of your home, on the lowest floor, open all the windows. Now, on the top level, south side, open the windows. The cooler, northside air will enter the house, force the warmer room air up and out the south-facing window.

You can enhance that effect by draping wet sheets over the outside of the open north-facing windows and keeping them wet. This is especially effective in low-humidity areas.

### Wash Your House

Another trick is to hose down the exterior of your house on particularly hot days. As the water evaporates, it draws heat out of the building.

Those are some ideas to keep you cool. Now for some *bright* ideas—

# —YOU LIGHT UP MY HOUSE: LIGHTING

Up to a quarter of your home electric bill goes to light up your house. I'm not recommending that you turn off all the lights, use candles and fumble around in the dark, but it's a safe bet that if you're like most homeowners, there are substantial savings you can make in lighting without living amid dark shadows.

A few simple rules will cost you nothing and save you something:

- Turn off lights when you leave a room. A 50-watt bulb left burning for a full year can cost you $25.
- Reduce overall lighting in non-working spaces of your home. Use only two incandescent bulbs in three-bulb fixtures.
- Buy table lamps that use three-way bulbs of 50-100-150 watts.
- Avoid long-life incandescent bulbs in most fixtures—they're less energy efficient.
- Keep lamps, bulbs and light fixtures clean—they'll shed more light and you'll be less tempted to turn on additional lamps.

### Be Lumen-Wise

If you're like most people, you buy your light bulbs by the watt. But wattage is a measurement of how much electricity a bulb uses, not how much light it gives off. Light values are measured in lumens, not watts. And it is possible that you'll be able to get more lumens (more light) with some lower wattage bulbs than with some higher-wattage bulbs. That means more light, even though you're burning less electricity.

The lumen value of a light bulb is printed on the carton. So it pays to compare different brands and different models of bulbs made by one manufacturer to get the most lumens per watt.

Maybe someday we'll all buy our bulbs by lumens, not by watts ("Hey, I need an 1800-lumen bulb—what's the lowest wattage that'll give me that much light?"), but for now it's buyer-beware.

**Watt Did You Say?** A large-wattage bulb *can* be more economical. A single 100-watt bulb may well give off more lumens than two 50-watt bulbs (and you also save the price of the second

## HOW MUCH WILL I SAVE?

Your saving will vary, depending on your electric rate and on the amount of usage your lights get. But, for every ten watts reduction, you will probably realize a yearly savings of $4 (plus the purchase price of all those second bulbs).

## FLUORESCENTS

Now that you understand lumens, you'll understand why

| Bulbs to replace | Average lumens per bulb | Lumens for two | Replace with | Lumens | Watt saving |
|---|---|---|---|---|---|
| 2 25-watt | 212 | 424 | 1 40-watt | 440 | 10 |
| 2 40-watt | 440 | 880 | 1 60-watt | 870 | 20 |
| 2 50-watt | 490 | 980 | 1 75-watt | 1200 | 25 |
| 2 60-watt | 870 | 1740 | 1 100-watt | 1750 | 20 |
| 2 75-watt | 1200 | 2400 | 1 100-watt | 1750 | 50 |

bulb). Here is a chart indicating, in general terms, how you can replace two smaller bulbs with a single, larger bulb and get equivalent lumens burning fewer watts. (Again, this is merely a guide and you *must* check the lumens value on the carton to be sure you're effecting an economy.)

fluorescent light fixtures can save you a lot of money. Quite simply, fluorescents deliver up to four times the lumens per watt as incandescent bulbs. For example, you can get the same lighting values from a 25-watt fluorescent bulb as from a 100-watt incandescent bulb. Your saving would be 75 watts—or about $30 a year. So in a couple of years you can pay for the fluorescent fixture.

## LONGER-LASTING, TOO

Fluorescent bulbs cost more than incandescent bulbs, but they last five to 26 times longer!

## Here's A Switch

Actually, here are two switches. Two switches that can save you money. A timer switch and a dimmer switch.

Timer switches cost about $12 and are extremely useful in basements or attics — areas of the house visited only occasionally, where a light could

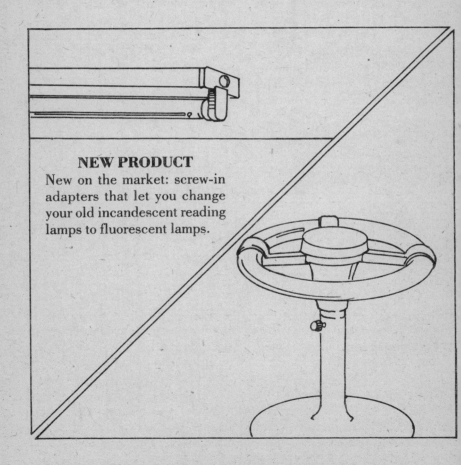

**NEW PRODUCT**
New on the market: screw-in adapters that let you change your old incandescent reading lamps to fluorescent lamps.

*Flourescent kitchen fixture, above and retrofit flourescent table lamp, below.*

accidentally be left burning for many days — or even months.

These switches are easy to install — but *be sure you cut off the circuit to the switch before you begin working!* Most common timers can be switched on for as long as an hour and will turn themselves off after that period. For children's playrooms or family rooms, you can buy four- or five-hour timer switches.

Not all dimmer switches are energy-savers. The older models dimmed light, but you still burned the same number of watts. Newer, solid-state dimmers *do* save energy. Be sure you read the label of any dimmer you buy to see that it is an energy-saving model and that it is Underwriters Laboratories

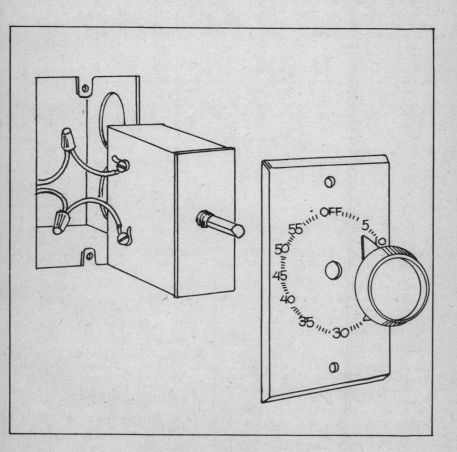

*Install a timer switch in seldom-used rooms and areas.*

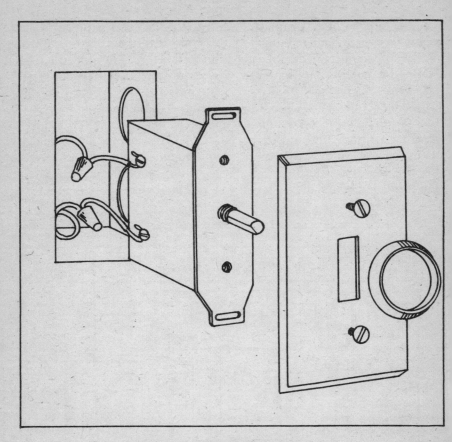

*Install energy-saving solid-state dimmer switches.*

listed. Again, when installing a dimmer switch, don't forget to cut off power to the switch before you begin working. If you don't, the results can be *shocking*!

## FRINGE BENEFIT

An added benefit—bulbs last longer when used at less than full intensity with a dimmer switch.

## HOW MUCH WILL IT COST?

Solid state dimmer switches cost between $8 and $12.

## HOW MUCH WILL I SAVE

About $10 per year per 100-watt bulb controlled by the dimmer switch.

## Daylight

It may sound obvious, but why not let the sun shine in? Sunlight's free and if you open your curtains, drapes, shutters, blinds and shades during daylight hours, you'll turn on fewer electric lights. (And keep those windows clean — a clean window, like a clean lighting fixture, gives you more light).

## The Shape Of Things To Come

New, more energy-efficient types of bulbs are on the way. The strange-shaped Halarc bulb should be on the market soon. Its developers claim it's five times more energy-efficient than an incandescent bulb and its screws right into your present light sockets. Also on the way soon is the internal reflective bulb. This bulb uses the natural heat of an incandescent filament to generate more light.

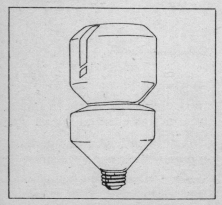

*The new Halarc bulb.*

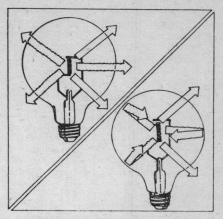

*Normal bulb, above, allows heat to dissipate out. Internal reflective bulbs, below, reflect heat back to the filament, keeping it bright while using less energy.*

# IF YOU CAN STAND THE HEAT, STAY IN THE KITCHEN

Your kitchen appliances use a fair amount of electricity and/or gas. You can save money by following a few simple tips for each unit:

## Refrigerator

- A refrigerator is a refrigerator, not a television set. There's no entertainment going on behind that door, so don't stand there with it open, gazing in and waiting for your favorite singing group to appear. And teach your children to open the door, take what they want quickly and close it after them.
- Dollar bill test. If the gasket around the refrigerator door isn't tight, cold air escapes and

**117**

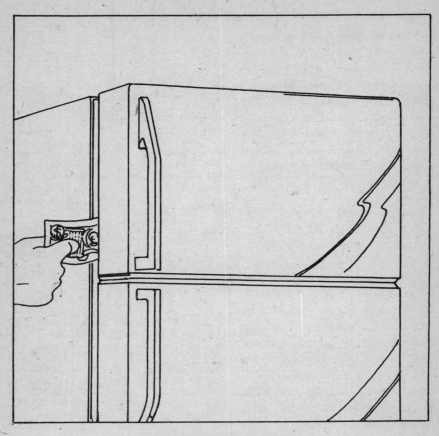

*If a dollar bill easily pulls out of your closed refrigerator door, your gasket is too loose.*

the refrigerator's motors have to work longer (which cost you more). Take a dollar bill, close it in the refrigerator and see if it pulls out easily. If it does, your unit needs a new gasket.

• Defrost! If you've got a manual-defrost refrigerator, defrost it. A quarter-inch build-up of ice puts a sizable load on your compressor motor.

• Buy two thermometers for your refrigerator — put one in the freezer, the other in the food compartment. Ideal temperatures are 40°F in the food area, 0-5°F in the freezer compartment. Any colder settings are simply a waste of money.

*Buy two thermometers for your refrigerator to be sure temperature is no colder than necessary.*

## BUYING A NEW REFRIGERATOR?

Check the EER and look for a higher-rated model. Avoid frost-free refrigerators; they use 50 percent more electricity than manual-defrost units. Refrigerators with the freezer on top or on bottom are more economical to operate than those which have the freezer alongside the food compartment. Also, ice-making refrigerators use more electricity. And, when installing your new refrigerator, put it in the coolest spot in the kitchen to reduce its workload as much as possible.

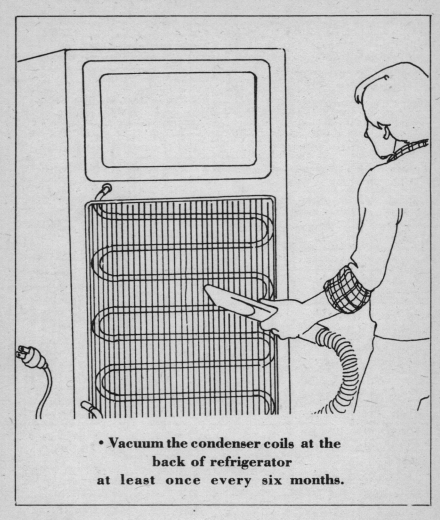

• **Vacuum the condenser coils at the
back of refrigerator
at least once every six months.**

## Your Range

- When cooking, don't allow the gas flame to burn up around edges of a pot—you're wasting precious gas. Keep the flame under the pot. With electric ranges, use small coils for small pots.
- Put a lid on it! When you want to boil water, put the lid on the pot. It'll boil faster and cost less in cooking gas or electricity.
- Keep your range top clean. Clean reflectors and burners work more efficiently.
- When cooking on an electric range, turn off the power before

the cooking time is up. The coils will retain enough heat to finish the job and you won't use as much electricity.

- Steam, don't boil vegetables. It uses less energy and they taste better and retain more nutrients.
- A microwave oven uses less energy than an electric oven, although the initial purchase price is quite high.
- Small electric appliances—toaster-ovens, electric fry pans and grills—are more economical for preparing small meals and snacks.
- Don't look. Your oven isn't a television set. Don't keep popping the door open to look for entertainment—you'll just be wasting the heat and slowing down the cooking time.
- Cook items together in the oven. Prepare tomorrow's casserole with today's roast and you'll only have to cook once, instead of twice. (That'll save *your* energy, too).
- One third of the gas used in our ranges goes to keep the pilot light burning. There are electric ignition devices on the market that allow you to turn the pilot off. BUT *DON'T* DO IT YOURSELF. YOU COULD EXPOSE YOURSELF TO DEADLY GAS. BE SURE YOUR GAS UTILITY TURNS OFF YOUR PILOT LIGHT.

## BUYING A NEW RANGE?

Look for one of the new gas models with electronic ignition systems (no pilot light). If you're in the market for an electric range, check the EER and buy an economical one. And consider buying a unit with a built-in microwave oven.

### Washing Dishes

- When washing by hand, don't run hot water over all the dishes—it wastes energy. Fill the basin, wash the dishes and then rinse.
- If you've got an automatic dishwasher, use the air dry cycle rather than the electrically heated drying cycle. If your dishwasher has no such cycle, open the door after the rinse cycle and let the dishes dry by evaporation.
- Use your dishwasher only when it's fully loaded. If it's only half-full, but there are no clean coffee cups or glasses left in the cupboard, take one out and wash it by hand. Don't be lazy, you can save a lot by running the washer only when it's full.

### Monday Is Wash Day?

Washing and ironing clothes is no longer a Monday-only activity. Here are a few tips to save energy (and money) any day of the week in the laundry:

- Fill that washer. One full load uses half the energy of two partial loads—both in hot water and in current to run the machine. Also, your washer will last longer if it runs fewer times per year.
- Try to do cold- or warm-water washes, rather than hot-water washes. Some garments can be rinsed in cold water—if you have clothing like that, don't waste hot water on it.

## WHAT ABOUT HEATING WITH YOUR DRYER?

A number of devices are on the market which divert the hot air from your dryer's exhaust into your home. They also divert lint into your home and, in gas models, could present a carbon dioxide danger. I don't recommend them. A dryer is for drying clothes, not for heating homes.

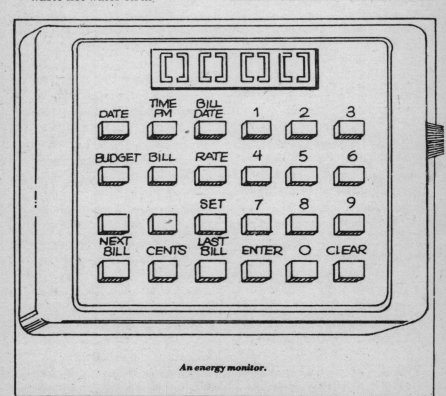

*An energy monitor.*

- Presoak extremely dirty clothing, so you won't have to wash twice.
- Hang your wash out to dry on a clothesline on nice days. You'll save energy and your wash will smell fresher.

How much energy can these steps save? How much are you wasting now if you're not following them? If you *really* want to know, look into—

## —ENERGY MONITORS

The energy monitor is a relatively new device which can be installed in your kitchen or basement and can tell you moment-by-moment how much electricity your household is using in terms of cost per hour in dollars and cents. A monitor costs more than $100 but it can probably scare you into cutting back on your consumption enough to pay for itself in a year's time.

Have you decided to enlist in the war on energy waste? Remember, your—

# —UNCLE SAM WANTS YOU:

# Tax Credits

**O**ur government is making energy conservation worth your while by doing a little something to help finance your energy-saving improvements.

In addition to saving money on your fuel and utility bills, you can qualify for a credit on your income tax for certain energy-savers. Now, that's a *credit*, not a deduction. A credit is subtracted directly from the amount of tax you owe, reducing your taxes by the amount of that credit. (A $200 *credit* is worth $200 to you. A $200 *deduction* is worth only $50 to you if you're in the 25 percent bracket.)

There are two categories of residential energy tax credits: Conservation Credits and Renewable Energy Source Credits. The first is fifteen percent of the first $2,000 spent on energy-saving items. That works out to a maximum Conservation Credit of $300. This Energy Conservation Credit is for such improvements

as insulation, caulking, weatherstripping, storm doors and windows.

The second credit is thirty percent of the first $2,000, plus twenty percent of the next $8,000. This is for money spent on renewable energy sources, such as solar heating or electricity-generating windmills. The maximum Renewable Energy Source Credit works out to a whopping $2,200. But, of course, a solar heating unit is far more costly than caulking your windows.

The credits are for your primary residence only—sorry, no breaks for improving a vacation home—and apply whether you own or rent that home. Also, the limits are fixed. If you spend $2,000 on insulating and weatherstripping this year and take the full credit, you cannot—under present law—take an additional credit next year, even if you spend another $2,000 in eligible improvements.

## HOW DO I GET THE CREDIT?

You claim either type of energy tax credit on line 45 of your Form 1040 (the long form) after figuring the amount of the credit on Form 5695. Be sure you keep a copy of your Form 5695, as well as a copy of your 1040. Also, save all receipts for energy-saving devices and services.

### CAUTION
If you're in doubt about whether an improvement qualifies for a tax credit, contact your local Internal Revenue Service office or your tax preparer or accountant.

Here's a sample Form 5695 prepared by the IRS:

---

**Form 5695**
Department of the Treasury
Internal Revenue Service

## Energy Credits
► Attach to Form 1040.
► See Instructions on back.

**1979**
29

Name(s) as shown on Form 1040

Your social security number

Enter in the space below the address of your principal residence on which the credit is claimed if it is different from the address shown on Form 1040.

**Part I** Fill in your energy conservation costs (but do not include repair or maintenance costs). If you have an unused energy credit carryover from the previous tax year and no energy savings costs this year, skip to Part III, line 20.

Was your principal residence substantially completed before April 20, 1977? . . . . . . . . . . . . . . . . . . ☐ Yes ☐ No
If you checked "No," do not fill in Part I.

1 Energy Conservation Items:
a insulation . . . . . . . . . . . . . . . **1a** ............... ......
b Storm (or thermal) windows or doors . . . . . **1b** ............... ......
c Caulking or weatherstripping . . . . . . . . **1c** ............... ......
d Other items (list here) ----------------------------- ............... ......
----------------------------------------------------- ............... ......
----------------------------------------------------- ............... ......
----------------------------------------------------- ............... ......
----------------------------------------------------- ............... ......
----------------------------------------------------- ............... ......
----------------------------------------------------- **1d** _____ ____

126

2 Total (add lines 1a through 1d) . . . . . . . .   **2**

3 Maximum amount . . . . . . . . . . .   **3**

4 Enter the total energy conservation costs for this
   residence from your 1978 Form 5695, line 2 . . .   **4**

5 Subtract line 4 from line 3 . . . . . . . .   **5**

6 Enter the amount on line 2 or line 5,
   whichever is less . . . . . . . . . .   **6**

7 Enter 15% of line 6 . . . . . . . . . . .   **7**

**Part II**    **Fill in your renewable energy source costs (but do not include repair or maintenance costs).** If you have an unused energy credit carryover from the previous year and no energy savings costs this year, skip to Part III, line 20.

8 **Renewable Energy Source Items:**

  a Solar . . . . . . . . . . . . . . .   **8a**

  b Geothermal . . . . . . . . . . .   **8b**

  c Wind . . . . . . . . . . . . . . .   **8c**

9 **Total** (add lines 8a through 8c) . . . . . . .   **9**

10 Maximum amount . . . . . . . . . . .   **10**

11 Enter the total renewable energy course costs for this
    residence from your 1978 Form 5695, line 5 . . .   **11**

12 Subtract line 11 from line 10 . . . . . . .   **12**

13 Enter amount on line 9 or line 12, whichever is less .   **13**

14 Enter 20% of line 13 . . . . . . . . . .   **14**

15 Subtract amount on line 11 from $2,000.
    If zero or less, enter zero . . . . . . . .   **15**

16 Enter amount on line 13 or line 15,
    whichever is less . . . . . . . . . .   **16**

17 Enter 10% of line 16 . . . . . . . . . .   **17**

18 Add lines 14 and 17 . . . . . . . . . . .   **18**

**Part III**    **Fill in this part to figure the limitation**

19 Add line 7 and line 18. *If less than $10, enter zero* .   **19**

20 *Enter your unused energy credit carryover
    from the previous tax year* . . . . . . .   **20**

21 Add lines 19 and 20 . . . . . . . . . .   **21**

22 Enter the amount of tax shown on Form 1040,
    line 37 . . . . . . . . . . . . .   **22**

23 Add lines 38 through 44 from Form 1040
    and enter the total . . . . . . . . . .   **23**

24 Subtract line 23 from line 22. If zero or less,
    enter zero . . . . . . . . . . . . .   **24**

25 Residential energy credit. Enter the amount
    on line 21 or line 24, whichever is less. Also,
    enter this amount on Form 1040, line 45 . . . .   **25**

Form **5695** (1979)

For sale by the Superintendent of Documents, U.S. Government Printing Office
Washington, D.C. 20402—Stock Number 048-004-01697-4

☆ U.S. GOVERNMENT PRINTING OFFICE: 1979-311-369/1063

## NO, THEY DON'T PAY YOU

What if your credit exceeds your tax obligation? What if you qualify for a $1,000 credit and your total tax bill is $900? Does the IRS owe you $100? Sorry, it doesn't work that way. *But*, you can apply the $100 leftover credit to your next year's taxes.

## QUALIFYING ENERGY-SAVING IMPROVEMENTS

The items you claim for a credit must be new and effective and they must have a minimum three-year useful-life expectancy. Improvements eligible for tax credits and the pages on which they're discussed are:

- Home insulation, page 13
- Water-heater insulation, page 102
- Storm windows and doors, page 49
- Caulking or weatherstripping, page 40
- Automatic setback thermostats, page 65
- Furnace derating, page 77
- Automatic flue dampers, page 78

## SORRY 'BOUT THAT

Fluorescent lighting, wood-burning stoves, replacement boilers and furnaces do not qualify for a tax credit, although they will save you energy and may be worthwhile investments without any help from Uncle Sam.

## RENEWABLE ENERGY SOURCE CREDITS

This credit, which again applies only to improvements on your principal home, is for the installation of solar-heat collectors, electricity-generating windmills and geothermal wells. This equipment must have been built into your new home or added on to an older home *after* April 19, 1977. The items must be new when installed and expected to last a minimum of five years.

## SORRY 'BOUT THAT, AGAIN

Greenhouses, as described on page 61 do *not* qualify for the credit.

## LAWS CHANGE

Tax laws and regulations change. What I've just told you is based on the latest IRS information. However, many tax questions are not answered with

cut-and-dried "yes" or "no" replies. It will pay you to keep careful track of your energy-saving expenditures and to ask about every energy-saving improvement you install in your home.

With or without a tax credit, energy-saving is an investment guaranteed to pay dividends.

So—

# —AMERICA,

## GO FORTH
## AND SAVE ENERGY,
## MONEY
## —AND OUR COUNTRY!

# INDEX

# A

Acrylic polymeric caulking, 45
Aerators, 104
Air cleaners,
  electricity consumption of, 99
Air coniditioners, 106-9
  coils of, 108
  electricity consumption of, 97
  energy audit of, 8-9
  Energy Efficiency Rating (EER) of, 108
  fan settings on, 108
  filters of, 106-8, *107, 109*
  insulation of ducts of, 28, *28*
  servicing, 106-8, *107, 109*
  setback devices for, 65
  shading, 108, *109*
  turning off, 108
Air ducts
  of forced-air systems, 71, *71*
  insulation of, 28, *28*
  return, in forced-air and hot-air systems, 78, *79*, 80
  Air filters of forced-air systems, 71-72, *71, 72*
Air registers (or vents)
  cleaning, 73
  removing obstructions from, 69
  replacing, 71
Air valves on steam radiators, *74*, 74-75
"Aladdin's lamp," emergency, 94, *94*
Aluminum-backed vinyl roll weatherstripping for doors, 58, *58*
Anti-freeze, for power-failure emergencies, 92, 93
Appliances, 97-122
  electricity consumption of, 97-100
  Energy Efficiency Rating (EER) of, 101
  percentage of family energy budget spent on, 4
  power-failure emergencies and, 93
  *See also individual appliances*
Ash, as firewood, 89
Attic doors, weatherstripping, 59
Attic fans, 110
Attic floors, insulation of, 20, *21*
  R-values recommended for, 15
Attic insulation
  Cost of, 29

ductwork, 28, *28*
electrical equipment, cables, and wires, 27
installing, 25-29, *26-28*
lighting fixtures and, 27, *27*
measuring your present, 14
nails protruding through roofing boards and, 24
pipes and, 28, *28*
R-values recommended for, 15
savings from, 29
smoking as a fire hazard when installing, 27
trapdoors, 27, *27*
walkways, 28, *28*
vapor barriers and, 26, *26*, 27
ventilation and, 22, *26*, 26-27
Automatic flue damper
  for furnaces, 77-78, *77*
  tax credit for installing, 128
  for water heater, 104

# B

Baffles, hanging, 78, *79*
Basement, insulation of, *21*
  R-values recommended for, 15
Bathroom, energy audit of, 10
Baths, showering instead of taking, 104
Batts, 16, *17*
  installation of, in attic, 25-27, *26*
  installation of, in crawlspace, 31-33, *32, 33*
  with vapor barrier, 22, 24
  widths of, 24
Birch (white), as firewood, 89
Blankets, electric, 66
  electricity consumption of, 99
Blankets, insulation, 16, 22, 24
Blankets, for power-failure emergencies, 92-94, *94*
Blender, electricity consumption of, 98
Blinds, 46
Boards, insulation, 17, *17*
Boilers
  vertical, 78, *79*
  *See also* Furnaces

Boy Scout flashlights, 91-92, *92*
Broiler, electricity consumption of, 98
Bulb thresholds, 59, *59*
Bushes, 61
Butyl caulking, 45

# C

Candles, 94
Carving knife,
    electricity consumption of, 98
Caulking, 42-46
    amount needed, 42
    annual check of, 46
    characteristics of different types of,
        44-45
    cost of, 46
    garage doors and windows, 34
    lead-base, 46
    for loose window frames, 40
    paint over, 46
    savings from using, 46
    tax credit for applying, 128
    tools and materials needed for, 44
    where to put, 42, *43*
Cedar, as firewood, 89
Ceiling fans, 110, 111
Ceilings, "ghosts" on uninsulated, 15, *16*
Ceilings, insulation of
    R-values recommended for, 15
    where to install, 20, *21*
Cellulose insulation, 19
Central air conditioning
    filters of, 107-8
    setback devices for, 65
    *See also* Air conditioners
Chemical insulation, 16
    health hazards of, 17-18
Chimneys
    insulating around, 28, *28*
    for wood-burning stoves, 86-88
Clock, electricity consumption of, 100
Clogged filter indicator, 72, *72*
Clothes dryer, 122
    electricity consumption of, 98
Clothes washer, *see* Washing machine
Clothing
    lower indoor temperature and, 64
    for power-failure emergencies, 92, 93
Cocklofts, insulation of, 14-15, 24
Coffee maker,

electricity consumption of, 98
Conservation Credits, 125-28
Consumer Product Safety Commission
    17, 20
Contractors
    installation of automatic flue damper
        by, 78
    installation of windows or doors by, 55
Convection heating system, 62-63, *62*
Cooking range, *see* Range
Cord of wood, 88-89, 89
Cost of energy (heating bills),
    saving on, 3-4
    attic insulation and, 29
    automatic flue damper and, 78
    caulking and, 46
    crawlspace insulation and, 32
    energy-audit score and, 11
    exterior wall insulation and, 31
    insulation and, 14, 31, 32
    lighting and, 112
    relative humidity level and, 68
    storm windows and, 53
    turning down the thermostat and, 64
    weatherstripping and, 42
    wood as alternate-fuel and, 88-89
Crawlspaces, insulation of cost of, 32
    installation of, 31-33, *32, 33*
    R-values recommended for, 15
    ventilation and, 22
    where to install, 20, *21*
Cutoff valve in steam radiators, 73, *73*

# D

Damper, flue, *see* Flue damper
Daylight, 117
Deep fryer, electricity consumption of, 98
Dehumidifier,
    electricity consumption of, 99
Derating your furnace, 77
Dew, vapor barriers and, 22, *23*
Dimmer switches, 115-16, *116*
Dishwasher, 121
    electricity consumption of, 98
    power-failure emergencies and, 93
Dishwashing by hand, 121
Door bottoms
    shoes, bulb thresholds and
        interlocking thresholds, 59, *59*
    sweeps, 58-59, *59*

Door frames, insulation of, 31, *31*
  *See also* Caulking
Doors
  energy audit of, 8
  glass, for fireplaces, 82, *82*
  installation by a contractor, 55
  revolving, 54
  shutting, 54
  storm, *see* Storm doors
  vestibule, 54
  weatherstripping, *see* Weatherstripping
    doors
Down-filled parka, 13
Drapes, 46-47, *47*
Ducts (air ducts)
  of forced-air system, 71, *71*
  insulation of, 28, *28*
  return air, 78, *79*, 80
Dust mask, installing insulation and,
  25, 27

Energy costs, *see* Cost of energy
Energy Efficiency Rating (EER), 101
  of air conditioners, 108
Energy monitors, 122
Energy Quotient (EQ), 5
Energy tax credits, 125-29
Exchange heating system, 63
Exposure, treatment for, 94-95
Exterior walls, insulation of
  checking, 15
  cost of, 31
  finished walls, 29
  moisture-blocking effect of wallpaper or
    paint, 24
  R-values recommended for, 15
  savings in heating bill, 31
  seating arrangements and, 29
  unfinished walls, 29-30, *29, 30*
  where to install, 20, 21
Exterior walls, uninsulated:
  "ghosts" on, 15

# E

EER (Energy Efficiency Rating), 101
  of air conditioners, 108
Egg cooker, electricity consumption of, 99
Electrical appliances, *see* Appliances
Electrical cables and wires, attic insulation
  and, 27
Electrical conduits, insulation around, 28
Electrical equipment, attic insulation and,
  27
Electric outlets, insulation of, 30
Elm, as firewood, 89
Emergency, surviving without fuel in an,
  91-95
Energy audit, 5-11
  air conditioning and ventilation, 8-9
  bathroom, 10
  bonuses, 10-11
  heating, 5-7
  insulation, 7
  kitchen, 9-10
  laundry, 10
  lighting, 9
  score and possible savings, 11
  television, 9
  trees and shrubs, 10
  water heating and usage, 8
  windows and doors, 8

# F

Fans, 110-11
  electricity consumption of, 99
Faucets, leaky, 104
Felt strips, for weatherstripping
  windows, 40
Fiberglass insulation, 18
Fir, as firewood, 89
Fire-fighting equipment, 92
Fire ordinances, insulation and, 17
Fireplaces, 80-83, 92
  fiberglass for blocking flue of, 82
  flue damper of, *81*, 81-82
  glass doors or screens for, 82, *82*
  nuts for starting or reviving, 87, *87*
  as radiant heating system, 62, 63
  wood-stove insert for, 82-83, *83*
Firewood, 88-89
First-aid kit, 91
Flashlights, Boy Scout, 91-92, *92*
Floor joists, insulation of crawlspaces and,
  31-32, *32, 33*
Floor polisher, electricity consumption of,
  100
Floors, insulation of checking, 15
  R-values recommended for
    attic floors, 15
  where to install, 20, *21*

Flow restrictors, 104
Flue
    fireplace, 82
    wood-burning stove, 86

Flue damper
    automatic, for furnaces, 77-78, *77*
    automatic, for water heater, 104
    fireplace, *81*, 81-82
Fluorescent light, 113-14, *114*
Foam insulation, 17, *17*
Foam-rubber weatherstripping
    for windows, 40, *41*
    with wood backing, for doors, 57, *57*
Food, power-failure emergencies and, 91, 93
Forced-air heating system, 63
    air filters of, 71-72, *71*, *72*
    air registers (or vents) of, 69, 71, 73
    with built-in humidifier, *67*, 68
    ducts of, 71, *71*
    removing obstructions from ducts of, *68*, 69
    return air ducts in, 78, *79*, 80
Foundation vents, 33
Foundation walls, insulation of, 21, *21*
Freezer
    electricity consumption of, 98
    power-failure emergencies and, 93
Frying pan, electricity consumption of, 99
Fuel, heating
    percentage of family energy budget
        spent on, 4
    surviving in emergencies without, 91-95
    wood as, 88-89
    *See also* Cost of energy (heating bills), saving on
Furnaces
    automatic flue damper for, *77*, 77-78
    derating, 77
    ducts for returning air to, 78, *79*, 80
    hanging baffles for, 78, *79*
    tuneup of, 76-77

# G

Garage
    insulation of, 20, *21*, 34
    turning the heat off in, 65
    weatherstripping and caulking doors and
        windows of, 34

Geothermal wells, tax credit for, 128
Germicidal lamp, electricity consumption
    of, 100
"Ghosts," 15, *16*
Glass doors, fireplace, 82, *82*
Greenhouse, 61, *61*
Gypsum board, as vapor barrier, 29

# H

Hair dryer, electricity consumption of, 100
Halarc bulb, 117, *117*
Hanging baffles, 78, *79*
Hay, 61
Heater (portable), electricity consumption
    of, 99
Heat flow
    insulation as resistance to, 14
    *See also* Ventilation

Heating bills, *see* Cost of heating, saving on
Heating pad, electricity consumption of, 99
Heating systems
    alternate, for emergencies, 92
    convection, 62-63, *62*
    energy audit of, 5-7
    exchange, 63
    forced-air, *see* Forced-air heating
        systems
        hot-water, *see* Hot-water systems
    lubricating motors of, 70
    radiant, 62, *62*, 63
    removing obstructions from, 68-70
    selecting someone to inspect, repair, or
        upgrade, 80
    steam heat, *see* Steam heat systems
    *See also* Furnaces; Thermostats

Heating zones, R-values and, 14, 15
Heat lamp, electricity consumption of, 100
Hedges, 61
Hemlock, as firewood, 89
Hosing down your house, 112
Hot-air register, *see* Air registers
Hot-air systems, *see* Forced-air systems
Hot plate, electricity consumption of, 99

Hot water
    percentage of family energy budget
        spent on, 4
    *See also* Water heater
Hot water faucets, leaky, 104

Hot water pipes
  insulating, 103, *103*
  *See also* Water pipes
Hot-water systems, 63
  solar, 105
  *See also* Furnaces; Radiators
Humidifiers, 22, 66
  cleaning, 68
  cost of, 68
  forced-air system with built-in, 67, 68
  savings from using, 68
Humidity, relative, 67-68
Hypothermia, 65

# I

Insulated shades, 43, *48*
Insulation, 13-34
  attic, *see* Attic insulation
  of basement, 15, *21*
  batts, *see* Batts
  blankets, 16, 22, 24
  boards, 17, *17*
  buying tips, 17-18
  cellulose, 19
  chemical, 16-18
  of cocklofts, 14-15, 24
  corrosiveness of, 18
  of crawlspaces, *see* Crawlspaces,
    insulation of
  of door and window frames, 31, *31*
  of electric outlet and switch plates, 30
  energy audit of, 7
  fiberglass, 18
  fire and building ordinances and, 17
  fire-resistant, 18
  of floors, *see* Floors, insulation of
  foam, 17, *17*
  of garage, 20, *21*, 34
  of hot water pipes, 103, *103*
  inorganic, 16, 18
  installing, 22, 24-34, *26-33*
  as irritant or health hazard,
    17-18, 20, 28
  loose, 16, *17*, 26, *26*
  moisture-resistant, 18
  organic, 16, 19
  perlite, 19
  plasticfoam, 19
  residing your house and, 61

  as resistance to heat flow, 14
  rock-wool, 18
  rot-proof, 18
  R-values of, 13-15, 18-19
  siding backed with, 59
  square feet needed, 24
  tax credit for installing, 128
  tools and equipment for
    installing, 24-25, *25*
  of unused rooms, 33-34
  ureafoam, 19, 20
  urethane, 19
  vapor barriers and, *see* Vapor barriers
  ventilation and, *see under* Ventilation
  vermiculite, 19
  vermin-proof, 18
  of water heater, 102-3
  where to install, 18-20, *21*, 22
  *See also* Storm doors;
    Storm windows;
    Weatherstripping doors;
    Weatherstripping windows
Internal reflective bulbs, 117, *117*
Iron, electricity consumption of, 99

# K

Kitchen, energy audit of, 9-10
Knee walls, insulation of, 20, 21

# L

Lamps
  emergency, 94, *94*
  heat, electricity consumption of, 100
  sun, electricity consumption of, 100
Landscaping, *60*, 61
Latex caulking, 44
Laundry, energy audit of, 10
Lead-base caulk, 46
Light bulbs
  fluorescent, 113-14, *114*
  Halarc, 117, *117*
  internal reflective, 117, *117*
  lumen values of, 112-13
Lighting, 112-117
  attic insulation and, 27, *27*
  emergency, 91-92, 94, *94*

energy audit of, 9
fluorescent, 113-14, *114*
lumens and, 112-13
rules for saving on, 112
*See also* Switches
Lubrication of heating system's motors, 70
Lumens, 112-13

# M

Maple (sugar), 89
Masonry walls, unfinishes, 30
Microwave ovens, 99, 121
Mixer, electricity consumption of, 99
Moisture, vapor barriers and, 22, *23*
Moisture-resistant insulation, 18

# N

Nuts, for starting or reviving a
    fireplace fire, 87, *87*
Nitrile caulking, 45

# O

Oak, as firewood, 89
Oil burners
    tuneup of, 76-77
    *See also* Furnaces
Oil lamp, emergency, 94, *94*
Oven
    microwave, 99, 121
    *See also* Range

# P

Paint(ing)
    over caulking, 46
    moisture-blocking, 24
    radiators, 76
Parka, down-filled, 13
Perlite insulation, 19
Pilot light of ranges, 121
Pine (white), as firewood, 89

Pipes
    steam, banging in, 73
    water, *see* Water pipes
    wood-burning stove, 88
Plasticfoam insulation, 19
Plastic sheeting
    storm windows made of, 51-53, *52*
    as vapor barrier, 29-30, *30*
Polysulfide caulking, 45
Pressure-sensitive foam weatherstripping
    for doors, 55-56, *55*
    for windows, 40, *41*

# R

Radiant heating system, 62, *62*, 63
    *See also* Fireplaces;
        Wood-burning stoves
Radiator enclosures, 69, *69*
Radiators
    air valves on, *74*, 74-75
    banging sounds in, 73
    bleeding air out of, 75, *75*
    cleaning, 73
    convection and radiation of heat by, *69*
    painting, 76
    pitching, 73, *73*
    reflectors for, 70, *70*
Radio
    battery-powered, for emergencies, 92
    electricity consumption of, 100
Radio/record player, electricity
    consumption of, 100
Range, 120-21
    electricity consumption of, 98
Reflectors, radiator, 70, *70*
Refrigerator, 11-20, *118-20*
    buying a new, 119
    electricity consumption of, 98
    power-failure emergencies and, 93
Refrigerator/freezer, electricity
    consumption of, 98
Relative humidity, 67-68
Renewable Energy Source
    Credits, 125-28
Return air ducts, 78, *79*, 80
Roaster, electricity consumption of, 99
Rock-wool insulation, 18
Romans, ancient: heating system
    used by, 62-63, *62*

Roofing, 59
Roof rafters, insulation of, 20, *21*
Roofs, insulation of, 20, *21*
R-values, 13
　or different types of insulation
　　materials, 18-19
　heating zones and, 14, 15
　meaning of "R" in, 14
　recommended, 15

# S

Sandwich grill, electricity consumption
　of, 99
Sashes, 39-40, *39*
Saving on heating bills, *see* Cost of energy,
　saving on
Seating arrangements, 29
Setback devices, 65
Sewing machine, electricity consumption
　of, 100
Shades, 46-48
　insulated, 48, *48*
Shaver, electricity consumption of, 100
Shingles, 59
Shutters, 46
Siding, 59, 61
Silicone caulking, 44
Shower heads, aerators and flow restrictors
　for, 104

Showers, 104
Solar heating units, tax credit
　for, 125, 128
Solar hot water systems, 105
Spring metal weatherstripping
　for doors, 56, 57
　for windows, 40, *40*, 41
Spruce, as firewood, 89
Steam pipes, banging in, 73
Steam radiators, *see* Radiators
Steam heat systems, 63
　cutoff valve in, 73, *73*
　pitching of radiators in, 73, *73*
　*See also* Radiators
Storm doors, 49, 53
　between garage and house, 34
　installation of, 53
　safety glass or clear plastic, 53
　tax credit for installing, 128

Storm windows, 35
　anodized-or baked-enamel finish, 49
　bare aluminum, 49
　choosing between storm doors and, 53
　cleaning, 53
　combination, 50-51, *51*
　cost of, 53
　measuring, 50
　old, 54
　plastic sheeting, 51-53, *52*
　single-pane, 49-50
　strength and appearance of, 49
　tax credit for, 128
　weatherstripping, 49, 51
　weep holes in, 49, 54
　which windows to do first, 54
Stoves, wood-burning,
　*see* Wood-burning stoves
Sun lamp, electricity consumption of, 100
Sunlight, 117
Switches
　dimmer, 115-16, *116*
　timer, 114-15, *115*
Switch plates, insulation of, 30

# T

Tax credits, 125-29
Television
　electricity consumption of, 100
　energy audit of, 9
Thermostat, 63
　for attic fans, 110
　location of, 66
　medical reasons for not turning down, 65
　setback devices for, 65
　turning down your, 64
Threshold
　bulb, 59, *59*
　interlocking, 59
Timer switches, 114-15, *115*
Toaster, electricity consumption of, 99
Toothbrush, electricity consumption
　of, 100
Trapdoors, attic, 27, *27*
Trash compactor, electricity consumption
　of, 99
Trees, *60*, 61
　energy audit of, 10

# U

Ureafoam insulation
  (Urea Formaldehyde or UF foam)
    health hazards associated with, 20
R-values and characteristics of, 19
Urethane insulation, 19

# V

Vacuum cleaner, electricity consumption
    of, 100
Vapor barriers, 22, *23*, 24
    attic insulation and, 26, *26*
    for crawlspace insulation, 32
    patching tears in, 27
    for unfinished walls, 29-30, *30*
Vegetable oil caulking, 44
Ventilation
    attic insulation and, 22, *26*, 26-27
    crawlspace insulation and, 33, *33*
    energy audit of, 9
    of insulated areas, 22
    natural flow of, 111-12, *111 See also*
        Fans
Vent pipes, insulation around, 28, *28*
Vents
    air, *see* Air vents
Vermiculite insulation, 19
Vertical boilers, 78, *79*
Vestibule, as a cold-air lock, 54

# W

Waffle iron electricity consumption of, 99
Walkways, attic, 28, *28*
Wallpaper, moisture-blocking, 24
Walls, insulation of
    exterior walls, *see* Exterior walls,
        insulation of
    foundation walls, 21, *21*
    interior walls of unused rooms, 33-34
    knee walls, 20, *21*
    unfinished walls, 29-30, *29, 30*

Washing machines, 122
    cold-water washes, 105
    electricity consumption of, 98
    fully loading, 104-5
Waste disposer, electricity consumption
    of, 99
Water heaters, 101-5
    automatic flue damper for, 104
    buying, 105
    cleaning heating elements of, 103-4
    draining sediment from, 103, *103*
    electricity consumption of, 98
    energy audit of, 8
    insulation of, 102-3, *103*
    lowering temperature of, 101-2
    percentage of home energy used by, 101
Water pipes
    insulating around, 28, *28*, 30, *30*
    insulation of hot-water pipes, 103, *103*
    power-failure emergencies and, 92, 93
Water supply, emergency, 91
Water temperature, lowering 101-2
Weatherstripping doors, 54-59
    aluminum-backed vinyl roll, 58, *58*
    annual check of, 42
    attic doors, 59
    clean, 58
    cost of, 42
    foam-rubber with wood backing, 57, *57*
    garage doors, 34
    pressure-sensitive foam, 55-56, *55*
    savings on heating bill, 42
    spring metal, 56, *57*
    storm doors, 53
Weatherstripping windows, 40-42, *40, 41*
    annual check of, 42
    cost of, 42
    savings on heating bill, 42
    storm windows, 49, 51
Weep holes in storm windows, 49, 54
Windmills, tax credit for, 125, 128
Window frames
    fixing loose, 40
    insulation of, 31
Window latches, 38, *38*
Window panes, broken, 36-37, *37*
Windows, 34-46
    cleaning, 35

energy audit of, 8
inspecting your, 35-36, *36*
installation by a contractor, 55
as solar collectors, 35
storm, *see* Storm windows
testing for air leaks around, 36
weatherstripping, 40-42, *40, 41*
Window sashes, 39-40, *39*
Window shades, 46-48

insulated, 48, *48*
Wood as fuel, 88-89
Wood-burning stoves, 83-88, 92
convection-and radiant-heat, 85, *86*
radiant-heat, 84-85, *85*
safety tips for, 86-88
Wood-stove fireplace insert, 82-83, *83*
Wool clothing, 92

# Monthly Energy Expenses

Before Energy-Saving Improvements

| 198___ | Jan. | Feb. | March | April | May | June | July | Aug. | Sept. | Oct. | Nov. | Dec. |
|---|---|---|---|---|---|---|---|---|---|---|---|---|
| Electric | | | | | | | | | | | | |
| Gas | | | | | | | | | | | | |
| Fuel | | | | | | | | | | | | |
| Other | | | | | | | | | | | | |

# Monthly Energy Expenses

Before Energy-Saving Improvements

| 198— | Jan. | Feb. | March | April | May | June | July | Aug. | Sept. | Oct. | Nov. | Dec. |
|---|---|---|---|---|---|---|---|---|---|---|---|---|
| Electric | | | | | | | | | | | | |
| Gas | | | | | | | | | | | | |
| Fuel | | | | | | | | | | | | |
| Other | | | | | | | | | | | | |

# See What You Save

## Monthly Energy Expenses
### After Energy-Saving Improvements

| 198__ | Jan. | Feb. | March | April | May | June | July | Aug. | Sept. | Oct. | Nov. | Dec. |
|---|---|---|---|---|---|---|---|---|---|---|---|---|
| Electric | | | | | | | | | | | | |
| Gas | | | | | | | | | | | | |
| Fuel | | | | | | | | | | | | |
| Other | | | | | | | | | | | | |

# Monthly Energy Expenses

Before Energy-Saving Improvements

| 198__ | Jan. | Feb. | March | April | May | June | July | Aug. | Sept. | Oct. | Nov. | Dec. |
|---|---|---|---|---|---|---|---|---|---|---|---|---|
| Electric | | | | | | | | | | | | |
| Gas | | | | | | | | | | | | |
| Fuel | | | | | | | | | | | | |
| Other | | | | | | | | | | | | |